Praise for Forest High

The stories are wonderful and beautifully written, with insights into the interior of a parallel, minimalist universe of the every-day. What makes these stories ultimately so arresting is how they capture the quiet, unspoken fears, the normalcy of unfinished relationships, and the inner strength it takes to face each day. The quietness of the stories belies their energy and the resilience of the characters which becomes a moving celebration of the human spirit.

–Milos Stehlik
Critic for Worldview on WBEZ/Chicago Public Radio

In a time when the importance of teachers has been unfairly challenged, Bob Boone gives us a collection of simply told, hard-edged tales from the lives of educators and their students. These rich, multifaceted stories ring true with details gleaned over the course of a full life. Reading them, one feels as if they are entering another version of our familiar reality, where secrets thrive in quiet classrooms and a passionate love of the pitfalls and victories of teaching motivates the creation of narrative.

–Lisa Locascio, *University of Southern California*
Recipient of the 2011 John Steinbeck Award for Fiction

Praise for Forest High

Bob Boone might be Chicago's most famous teacher. Since the 1960s he's been educating youth of Chicago and its suburbs, as well as those in New York and Germany. In 1991, he founded the terrific Young Chicago Authors program, a forum for creative writing and performance among teens, earning him an invite to the White House by Michelle Obama, and a *Chicagoan of the Year* nod by Chicago magazine in 2002.

While continuing to teach, Mr. Boone has also found time to pen a few textbooks, a teaching memoir and now *Forest High*—a *Winesburg, Ohio*-esque cycle of nine loosely related short stories centering on the eponymous fictional high school. They are not flashy stories, nor are they without flaws. But Mr. Boone knows how to spin a yarn, and each one in this—his first book of fiction—is a yarn worth spinning. They are stories about teachers and students, though who fits which role isn't always clear. We have second-generation educators, the angsty children of angsty parents, kids who have graduated to wildly different futures.

The best of the bunch is *Funny in the Summer,* about the burgeoning friendship between two teachers—one in his sixties, the other in her twenties—that might be heading toward something more. Like all of Boone's stories, it wedges itself between the things we understand to find meaning in the space between.

The Caddy, the last story in the collection, is exceptional, too. The story of two thirty-two-year-old Forest High graduates—one who goes on to Princeton and a career in finance, and another who goes to work a thankless job at a country club—is wonderfully enigmatic due to the shaky first-person narration by the title character, who understands far less of what's going on than we do.

Praise for Forest High

Boone's trouble, however, is the occasional slouch into 101-level creative writing boo-boos. He has a proclivity for giving exposition through dialogue, and he tends to wrap up stories too neatly, letting sentimentality poke its head into the frame.

That said, these minor grievances do not by any means torpedo this fine book, and are far outweighed by its strengths. Namely, the three-dimensional portraits of teachers and students, their twining fates, bound in solidly constructed, realist narratives—ones that sparkle with the feeling of lived experience.

–Eric Lutz
Newcity Lit

Implicit in these tales are basic human questions: what does it mean to be a good teacher or a good person? What, for that matter, is meant by the phrase 'good school'? In this age of standardized tests and the relentless attempt at quantifying students and teachers alike, Bob's stories offer a refreshingly human portrayal of his characters. He never fails to see the comedy in the conflict between the conventional and unconventional, and he portrays his characters with nothing less than a sympathetic eye. In these stories, Bob always looks beyond the Forest to the individual trees.

–John O'Connor, Author, 'Wordplaygrounds'
Teacher at New Trier High School

Praise for Forest High

The most moving stories focus on aging instructors and their legacies, after having influenced the lives of coworkers and pupils, for better or worse. *Funny in the Summer* centers on the relationship between Armand, a veteran educator approaching retirement, and Julie, a younger instructor who presses him to share humorous memories from his long career. However, Boone does not glorify all teachers as laudable role models or paragons of organization. *Special Project* presents the power struggle between two characters with equally lackluster records: Jerome, a chronically absent student with few completed assignments, and Arthur, an English teacher with poor judgment who forgets that Jerome is enrolled in his class. When grades are due, Arthur attempts to negotiate a mutually beneficial agreement and alter his grade book by hand. Boone's economical use of dialogue serves a dual purpose, as characters reveal questionable attitudes in a small amount of space or, more often, withhold uncomfortable truths from themselves and others. These layered, often humorous classroom insights are buoyed by the author's lean, clear writing style.

The author will find an eager audience among readers who work in the profession, but these stories are genuinely accessible for any student who has ever wondered what's happening on the other side of the desk.

–Kirkus Indie Review

Praise for Forest High

Bob Boone gives us an insider's view into the world of Forest High. These stories are spare, terse and capture the quirkiness of characters and circumstance utterly consistent with the world of schools—a world where, as Boone well knows, every story implies another. An astute observer, Bob Boone writes with humor, compassion and insight.

–*Larry Starzec, Fiction Editor, 'Willow Review'*
Professor of English at College of Lake County

These aren't your typical teacher stories. In the living and breathing world of brick, glass and glue sticks, we want our teachers to leave their real lives—their darknesses, their longings, their secrets and desires—back at their desks and locked in their lockers in the faculty room. But this is Bob Boone's school. There is no safe place here for the containment of these things. The best Boone's characters can do is take off their jackets at the door, empty the pockets of their pants—their shreds and crumplings, their histories and regret, their hearts and longings—stuff it all in the pockets and sleeves of their jackets, drape their coats over the backs of their chairs, and just like the rest of us, cross their fingers and pray to God that nothing falls out before the bell rings.

–*Billy Lombardo, Author, 'The Man with Two Arms'*
Recipient of the 2011 Nelson Algren Award for the Short Story

Books by Bob Boone

Forest High
AMIKA PRESS

Moe's Cafe: 48 Decidedly Different Creative Writing Prompts
GOOD YEAR BOOKS

Inside Job: A Life of Teaching
PUDDIN'HEAD PRESS

Developing Your Test-Taking Skills
NATIONAL TEXTBOOK COMPANY

Language and Literature
ED., MCDOUGAL LITTELL, INC

Verbal Review and Workbook for the SAT
HARCOURT BRACE JOVANOVICH PUBLISHERS

Hack
FOLLETT PUBLISHING COMPANY

Using Media
PEACOCK PRESS

Forest High

Forest High

SHORT STORIES BY

Bob Boone

Coach first appeared in *Confluence,* © 2000
Funny in the Summer first appeared in *New Scriptor,* © 2009

First Edition   ISBN 13: 978-0-9708416-6-7
AMIKA PRESS   466 Central AVE #23 Northfield IL 60093   847 920 8084
info@amikapress.com   Available for purchase on amikapress.com
Cover art by Krista Franklin, kristafranklin.com. Back cover photograph by Enrica
Mattioli. Author photograph by Sue Boone. Designed and typeset by Sarah Koz. Body
in Dante MT, designed by Giovanni Mardersteig and Charles Malin in 1955, digitized by
Ron Carpenter, 1993. Titles in Benton Sans Condensed Light, designed by Cyrus High-
smith and Tobias Frere-Jones, 2000. Thanks to Nathan Matteson.

For Sue

Contents

Chairman Mildred

Billy Oates stood staring for the last time at the words on the mailbox: MILDRED HOPKINS, ENGLISH DEPARTMENT CHAIRMAN. How many thousands of times, he wondered, had she reached her hand into that slot for the daily bulletin, for the compositions, the catalogues, and for all that other stuff that filled her life? And such a big hand it was, too. Alan Clovis, his old buddy from the English department, had joked under his breath that Mildred needed the larger slot because her hand would not fit into the standard slot assigned to regular staff. Cruel, but true. Mildred was a large lady.

Every day, she'd reach into this slot, gather up the mail in one hand, slide it into her briefcase, and then head down the hall to her office, nodding to but never bantering with people she passed. Bantering was definitely not her style. Just as it was not her style to say 'Chairperson.' She was and always would be a 'Chairman.' Or better yet, 'The Chairman.'

Billy looked around at the main office filled with empty desks, surrounded by walls with empty bulletin boards and a few animal posters and doors leading into the administrative offices. The counter, usually covered with stacks of paper, was completely bare. Empty flowerpots lined the window ledge. In a month, at the start of school, they would be brimming with roses and other flowers, and there would be people here: secretaries, well-tanned teachers, a few rested students. Don Lewis would have taken over as chairman. Don was Mildred's choice— a smart, quiet, single fellow. And well organized. By dying in the summer, Mildred had provided for a smooth transition for her

successor. And soon her name would be peeled off the mailbox
and Don's would replace it.

To an outsider, it all might seem like meaningless stuff—
a meaningless title in a meaningless department. To people like
Mildred, Clovis, Don Lewis, and Billy, nothing else really mattered. And to Mildred, it mattered the most of all. She viewed
her teachers as an enlightened army, holding back the advancing
stupidity of the school administration. "Morons," she would
mutter at meetings. "Ex-coaches and ex-Drivers' Education
instructors. All morons. They're not going to tell us what to
teach." And they didn't; Chairman Mildred terrified them.

Billy had started at Forest High in 1972. Then, as now, Forest was a middle-size high school in a middle-size town, and it
seemed to fit his middle-size aspirations perfectly. A shy son of
Iowa teachers, he was looking for a place where he could fit in,
and with his teacher genes, respect for books, and modest suc-
cess in his first job the previous year, he figured he had a good
chance to make it at a school like Forest.

He met Mildred at the very first Forest High School English
department meeting, which was held in her classroom. The
desks were in a semi-circle facing front. Coffee and juice and
rolls were on a table in the rear, and that's where they had their
first conversation. She welcomed him with a firm handshake.
He congratulated her on being promoted to chairman. She
nodded down at him cordially. "I hope this new job won't get in
the way of my teaching." And then she excused herself to greet
the other teachers. He checked out some of the posters, one
of Oscar Wilde with the quote: 'Some people bring happiness
wherever they go, others whenever they go.' On the board was
another quote—perhaps for her first class. It was from Emerson:
'Foolish Consistency is the hobgoblin of little minds.'

She controlled the meeting that day, covering schedules, unexplained absences, fire drills, conferences, grades, textbooks, conventions. She told the people what they needed to know. She answered questions efficiently. She laughed politely at a couple of jokes by a teacher sitting next to Billy but moved the meeting forward. Forty minutes later the meeting was over. "Go get yourselves some lunch and spend all the time you need on planning your first classes. I'll be around if you have any questions. And please remember," she paused, and then in a clear voice without a trace of irony provided some parting words: "Take your job seriously." As Billy thought about it then and often later, it was such an odd and wonderful thing for a new leader to say.

Billy ate downstairs and was joined by Clovis, the jokester at the meeting. He introduced himself as the department fuck-up. "I'm afraid," he said, "our chairman's words were aimed at me. Well, you know something? She's right. I can be irreverent. What's your story?"

Billy told him about his job in Iowa. A good place to start, he explained, but too small and not a happy place. But he liked the kids. He decided he wanted to be near a big city and not in one. Forest was the place. "I am a teacher's kid, after all."

After lunch, Billy returned to his classroom and studied the sophomore curriculum one more time. It was clear and sensible. The year would start with short stories and then move to poetry and drama. The curriculum told him what to do, leaving ample room for his own ideas. The last words were, *Look for opportunities.* He noticed that one of the authors of the curriculum was Mildred Hopkins.

From the beginning, things felt good. His students, basically an average bunch, liked talking about the stories and writing about them. He could keep them quiet. He could make them laugh. He could connect what they were discussing to what was going on in their lives.

He made a point of staying on top of things, in part because he did not want Mildred coming after him. She observed his class in late October. The next day in his mailbox he found a short evaluation of his teaching: *Good questions. Make sure to include more kids in the discussion. Keep getting the papers back right away. It means more to the kids when they can see the results.*

The department meetings were short and infrequent. Mostly she would remind people of what was coming up. She pointed out an *Opportunity Board* she had for trips and special projects. And she never missed a chance to ridicule the administration. "We have a good curriculum and great teachers. I'm not going to let those yahoos add meaningless tasks. You worry about teaching, and I'll worry about them."

But still Billy was not quite comfortable around Mildred. From time to time he had tried to start up a conversation at lunch, but her short answers told him she had better things to do. She was never at the parties or the bar on Fridays or at the games. After his first year, he was pleased with his effort but still wary of Mildred.

When Billy entered the building the morning after he heard of Mildred's death, the hall was filled with desks all pushed together. The squeaks of a waxing machine in a distant hall was the only sound. He didn't see anyone, but he did smell the aroma from Rocco's cigar. The heavy air held on to the smoke. Without the kids tearing through the halls, it would stay there for a long time. Rocco—Mildred called him 'El Duce'—had been a janitor at Forest longer than Mildred had been a teacher. Rocco had fought with the Italians in the Second World War. Mildred had once asked him to be interviewed by one of her classes. She thought he had as much to offer as her other colleagues.

Billy got the news of Mildred's death the night before. Clovis had left a message on his answering machine. "Bad news, Billy. Mildred died this morning. Neighbors found her in her front yard. She had a heart attack while walking back to her apartment with her newspaper. Services are Saturday. We thought maybe you could say something."

Billy walked down the hall toward the classrooms. The custodians had finished waxing the floors in this hall, and the desks were out of view. He paused at the classroom where Mildred had taught for so long. Unlike some department chairmen who stayed away from the students, she always taught a full load of classes up until the last years, when her heart started to fail. But she did not quit. Last year, she'd taught three classes and picked up a fourth when young Tom Harris came down with mono.

When he reached the library, he stopped and looked in. There it was: 'Billy's table.' That's where he sat after school to grade papers. He had a key just in case the library was locked. He had started working there his second year, and he was still going strong. Next year he'd be back.

Mildred had joined him his third year. "They're painting my office. May I join you?" Before he could say "Sure," she sat down one table over, spread out her work, and began reading student papers. With her so close, he had a hard time concentrating. She was just too big for him. Her size, her pure volume, seemed to extend beyond her skin and consume the air around her.

She came back again a few days later and kept coming back. "I hope you don't mind. It's peaceful here. No telephone. Lots of books. You know how it is." Did he? Did he know how it is? Anyway, he did not mind her being there. And at some point he would have minded if she were not there.

Every so often, they chatted about the papers they were reading. Billy asked his students to write about the books they were reading and also about what they had done in their lives. And he gave them a chance to make up things and to write poetry. As long as they were writing, he was happy. Mildred, who encouraged this sort of thing, liked to hear what Billy's kids had to say. Her students were seniors. They spent more time analyzing and synthesizing works of literature. But she also gave them plenty of chances to express themselves.

But while the conversation was friendly and often informative, usually they didn't talk at all. And that's how it was for twenty-five years. Occasional talk about what their students were writing, nothing about the bozos in the office. Nothing about the boy with the gun, the girls who got pregnant, the football coach who had a gay lover in South Beach. Nothing about the state champion basketball team. Nothing about the graduate who became an astronaut. Nothing about the kilo of grass found in the class president's locker. Nothing about the changing atmosphere brought on by computers and the new emphasis on testing and No Child Left Behind. Nothing about who was doing what in the English department. Certainly not that, for Mildred had continued to be the strong, mildly intimidating, encouraging leader she had been from the start.

Other teachers, especially the chronic gossipers, knew how much time Billy and Mildred spent together. For most, this little unmarried man and this large unmarried woman belonged together, sitting at a table in a room full of books, purposefully working. Clovis, of course, had his own ideas. Once at a faculty party, he drunkenly eased up to Billy and quietly asked, "You're not humping her in there are you, Old Boy?" Billy had blanched and coughed and excused himself.

In this last year, Mildred clearly was failing. Her heart was weak; her energy gone; she had lost some control over her hands and could not write as well. She began to forget. At first

Billy refused to notice. She was, after all, invincible. But when she referred to Clovis as 'Cloris' and arrived late and confused at a meeting, he knew the person who had sat next to him for all those years was not the same.

And she knew that he knew. And they began to talk more. It was her way of reminding herself to keep her mind active. And one day she left a list in front of him. It was a short agenda for the meeting with spaces. She wanted him to fill in those spaces. He did so gladly. And as he helped her more, she relied on him more.

But the last day, she was sharp once again. The final meeting went smoothly. After the meeting, she found him in the library where he was writing a letter to a former student. "I have one more year, Billy, and then I leave. You'll be here, won't you?"

Of course.

Now three months later, he was imagining working alone in the library. He would try, but it might be too painful.

Time to go back home and write the funeral remarks. He knew what to include and what to leave out. Certainly he would leave out what had happened at a department meeting two years ago. At that meeting a new teacher mentioned having a review session in the library after school. Clovis beamed. "Not there, Patsy. That's where Mildred and her boyfriend hang out." It was a cute remark. A Clovis remark. It brought a few chuckles, but Billy, sitting across the table from Mildred, could see her blushing.

Second Chance

Mark Ward actually liked getting the classroom ready. Back at his old school, he had never done much with the classroom, but this time around, he might just do a few things with it. He wouldn't bring in flowers, but there was no reason he couldn't hang up posters of Hemingway and Crane and Woolf. And maybe the *Howl* poster with Alan Ginsburg's face superimposed over the first few stanzas. Maybe even some enlarged cartoons from *The New Yorker*. Forest High looked like the kind of school where teachers did that sort of thing.

He might even think about what to wear the first few days. For teaching, his dad always wore a sport coat or a certain sleeveless sweater that made him look like a teacher. Maybe Mark should do that. Then his blond curly hair and smooth kid-like face wouldn't be as obvious. He might even remove the earring.

But right now, before he did any serious decorating or thinking about his clothes, he'd better glance at the books and the curriculum to make sure he could at least get through the first few classes. That's what happens when they offer you a job at the end of the summer. You arrive totally unprepared. Nothing to do but cram. But he could do it. He wasn't afraid to work. He'd be able to come up with lesson plans. And when he had a classroom full of kids, he would do just fine. There was no question. He could teach. He liked making the classroom come alive. He left his old school for other reasons.

It was these 'other reasons' that mattered most right now, though. Maybe he should have defended himself more, but somehow he knew he got good advice. The department chairman had called. "Mark," he said, "we need to talk. Come to

Principal McBride's office tomorrow at noon." Old guys looking at a younger teacher. He had done nothing wrong all year.
Nothing. But it seemed he was using bad judgment. Reports of
going to student parties. Smoking in his car before school. Hang-
ing out with the teachers who weren't going anywhere. They
didn't use the words, but they could have: *bad crowd*. That's what
they meant. And they knew his family. That was big. They knew
his folks. The principal had gone to school with his dad. He had
spoken at the funeral for his parents: "So untimely; so tragic."

Then they had told him one more time what a strong teacher
he could become. He liked kids; he could get them to talk; he
could keep them quiet. Kids believed in his enthusiasm. Don't
waste this talent on scum. Don't waste it on those teachers who
have given up and would like nothing better than to pull you
down. Don't waste your time on those teachers who want to be
like the kids. Be a man. Grow up. We've already found another
job for you. You'd be a fool not to take it.

But still. It was weird to get this lecture in the summer and
then to move on to this school on the other side of the city.
They weren't right, but they weren't wrong. Shit, he was a
young guy. He was a big party guy in college, but who wasn't?
What was he supposed to do with his time?

Still he took their advice. They were giving him a second
chance, even though he hadn't really done anything wrong.

This new place should work for him. It was in the Chicago
area but farther north from his last place. But the students would
be the same—a lot of college-bound kids, a few blue-collar
types, and enough diversity so he didn't have to feel guilty. He'd
do fine here. He'd try to follow the rules and keep a neat room.

He was starting to make a list of things to do the first day
when into the room strolled a young teacher. She was wearing a
red sweatshirt and carrying a U.S. History textbook with yellow

sticky notes between the pages. She looked to be in her mid-twenties—just about Mark's age. She walked up to the desk and stood there smiling. Mark stared back and grinned. "I'm Mark, the new English teacher. Who are you?" He offered his hand. "So, you teach history?"

"I'm Lottie, and, yes, this is a history book."

She took his hand and held it longer than she needed to. She had olive skin and dark hair that was pulled back into a functional ponytail. She looked healthy, but not bony like a jock. She had a clean, handsome face and an easy smile, but her eyes told a different story. This person could keep her kids quiet. No doubt about that. And quite soon, maybe sooner than she would like, her features would harden and her posture would decline and she would look more like what she was—a teacher. He was a teacher's kid. He recognized things like that.

"So why did they hire you? I hear you were teaching across town. And now you're here teaching in Mrs. Abel's old room. Do tell...very mysterious. Want to share it with me?"

"When we have more time." He looked down at his work and continued writing.

She reached out and grabbed his list and turned it so she could read it. "What do we have here? 'Introductions, class plan, *What is English?*, discussion, and free writing.' Very good, Mark. It looks like you have enough here to keep the little fuckers busy."

"That's right." He couldn't believe it. School hadn't started and here he was with one of the teachers he was supposed to avoid. If anything she looked younger and wilder.

She looked at him with what could only be called a dirty smile. "Come on, Mark. Why'd you leave the last place? Nothing kinky, I hope."

"Nothing like that." He tried to be careful with his words. "I wasn't happy with the way things were going. I found out about the opening here. No big deal. No story. Just one more boring English teacher."

"That's it? Never got caught doing anything really dangerous?"

Her tone made him a little nervous. "Nope," he replied quickly. "My department chairman and the principal wrote great recommendations. What about you? What's your story?"

"You'll find out." She looked down at her book and gave an exaggerated yawn. "This is my fourth year here."

"Getting bored?" Mark wondered if she had a boyfriend. His last girlfriend dumped him after he quit his job. He figured someone new would come along, but not this soon.

"You finish what you're doing, Mark. I've got something to do over here." She walked quickly to the other side of the room and opened up the window. "I hope you'll put lots of flowers here just like Mrs. Abel did. She kept a beautiful classroom. Too bad about that bus."

Mark looked down to study his notes and then looked back up again and started shouting. "Hey, what are you doing?" He could not believe what he was looking at. Lottie was taking a deep drag on a joint and blowing the smoke out the window.

"Just enjoying myself," she said and took another drag. "Calm down, Mark. We're not in Victorian times, you know. Even teachers get stoned. There's no Big Brother watching."

He rushed over and pushed a chair in front of the door. Then he ran back and opened the rest of the windows. "This is my first day, for Christ's sake! You'll get me fired! And that's it! I'm out of teaching forever. Please, Lottie, put that goddamn thing out. Out! Out! Put that fucking thing out!"

But she didn't. Instead she laid it on the windowsill and reached over and grabbed Mark by the arm and pulled him towards her. For a moment he held back, but only for a moment. Suddenly, he was in her arms. "Just relax," she whispered and then kissed him. He resisted for only a second. And he didn't resist at all when she reached behind him for the joint and slipped it between his lips. "I grew it in my backyard. What do you think?"

He paused for just a moment and then took a deep drag. He hadn't been stoned for a month, and the pot tasted wonderful.

Then he was kissing her again and then pushing sideways and then flicking the joint out the window as he moved her towards the closet. *What the hell,* he kept saying to himself. *What the hell.*

"Mark, my goodness," she whispered to him. "Are you thinking of doing what I think you are? In the closet? On top of Mrs. Abel's coat? But we can't. You've got your department meeting, and I have to be someplace. But I'll be here all year." She wiggled free and started to walk away.

Halfway to the door, she stopped, turned around, and lifted up her sweatshirt. She wasn't wearing a bra. "Coming events, Markie. Coming events. See you soon." She pulled down the sweatshirt, grabbed her book and skipped out the door.

He wanted to chase after her or at least pause and savor the memory, but he had no time. Grinning and shaking his head, he turned on the fan and took one last look at his notes. How could this have happened on his first day of school? Were all the teachers here like Lottie? What kind of place was this?

The department meeting was held in a classroom down the hall. Most of the teachers appeared to be in their forties or fifties, but there were a few who looked younger than he was. The chairman was an angular, good-natured man named Lewis. He introduced Mark and the other new teacher to the group. Mark greeted his new colleagues and said he felt lucky to be teaching in a school like Forest. He said he was looking forward to helping out with the literary magazine. The other new teacher, an older fellow named Bassett, told the teachers he would be directing plays. He was also glad to be at Forest. He blinked a lot and chewed on his lower lip. "I told these two men," the chairman said with a grin, "that nothing matters more than motivation. Nothing."

Everyone nodded. The chairman then talked about his recent trip to England. In June he and his wife and seven Forest students had traveled to Cambridge, England, where they all took classes. "I can honestly say, people, this was one of the best experiences I have ever had as a teacher, and I know the kids felt the same way. So I'm going to have them tell you about what they learned this summer. This will be a good way for us to begin the year. We'll have plenty of time in the afternoon to talk about the curriculum." A few people actually applauded, and Mark, who was about to scribble a note to Lottie, joined in.

The chairman walked over to the door and opened it. Into the room filed several students. The first two to enter were clean-cut, confident-looking boys. Mark recognized the types. Some day soon, they would be Ivy Leaguers. Even though it was still August, they were wearing neckties. The third student marched through the door just as confidently, but she was dressed more casually. In fact, she was wearing a sweatshirt— a red sweatshirt.

Max the Terrorist

In August, two weeks before the start of my senior year, I got a call from Mr. Jerry Simpson. He wanted to meet for breakfast at this little dump of a place down near the empty warehouses. He had something important to ask me. This might have seemed strange because I'm a student and he's a history teacher and not even my teacher yet, but I liked the guy and figured he had his reasons.

Most people would say the most notable thing about me is my old man. Back in the early '90s, a few years before I was born, he made a name for himself protesting the first war in Iraq. He and some buddies marched around the state capital carrying signs. He wrote some articles and passed around petitions. The FBI investigated him and found out he had been in contact with former Vietnam radicals—old guys but still dangerous, or so they said. Now he teaches sociology part time at the community college and writes angry articles and letters that no one reads. He wears a ponytail and smokes a little pot. He's more like a roommate than a dad, but he's okay. I could do a lot worse.

My mom works as an administrator at the hospital in North Chicago. She spends a lot of time there, even at night and on weekends. She pays attention to my schoolwork but doesn't seem to care that I don't care. Like my dad, she doesn't seem to mind that I'm on my own. Also, I think she might have something going with one of the doctors.

I'm small and plain. Bad posture and oily hair. But I don't really care what I look like. My friends are the same way—small and unattractive. We sit around on weekends and make fun of all the assholes at school who think they're important. Not the bullies or jocks. They're simple to figure out. It's the school leaders who make us sick. The guys who act like adults. And I mean *act*. They carry iPhones and frown. They look for excuses to shake hands. I can't tell you how much we enjoy hating those people.

Simpson came to Forest a year ago. He was in his late twenties. He had been a coach or something and decided to teach and kind of fell into this job when it became open. But he must have done okay because they kept him on for this year. My dad had heard he was pretty good and seemed glad that he would be my teacher.

Word gets around in a school, and people said Simpson knew what he was talking about but didn't make a big deal about it. He asked good questions and kept the class awake. He didn't fill papers with comments, but what he wrote made sense.

I had a class right next to his, and he'd joke around with me in the hall. He said he had heard of my old man and admired him. And I could tell he meant it. He asked me about politics sometimes. So I guess you could say we were kind of buddies without really knowing each other.

Greta's is a 24-hour place. You'll see boozers sobering up and construction guys getting ready to go to work in the early morning. Just about everyone smokes. My dad comes here when he wants to pretend he's working class. I didn't have to meet Simpson as early as the guys on their way to building sites.

Simpson was sitting at a table in the far corner scribbling something onto a yellow pad. He was wearing an old stained blue sweatshirt. But he's a blond, athletic guy and still looked better than the rest of the losers in this place.

A waitress with serious cleavage and strong perfume followed me to the table. She waited for me to order, and I told her toast and a coke. Simpson winced and laughed and then asked me about my summer and my college plans. I told him about my job at the stationery store and that even after graduation I was going to stay away from school until I figured out what I wanted to do. Maybe a couple of classes at the community college, but that would be it. He said more people should do that. I told him I was looking forward to having him as my teacher in the coming year. And he thanked me.

Then he sat there looking off to the side where an old couple was sharing scrambled eggs and a huge order of bacon. He was tapping his finger on the table. This was not the relaxed guy who liked to joke with me in the hall. He actually took a deep breath, stared at his hands and looked right back at me. "Max, I called you because I need to know about the demonstration at graduation last June. What do you know?"

It seemed like an odd thing to ask, but he wouldn't have gone to all this trouble of meeting at this shithole without a good reason. "I wasn't there," I said, "but a friend who had a good view told me that at the end of the ceremony, Superintendent Kiefer was at the podium sucking up to the parents and grandparents. The graduates were on the stage behind him. Then all of a sudden about ten of the graduates held up signs that read STOP THE KILLING IN AFGHANISTAN! A few others had signs with pictures of blood and gore and weapons. One big kid acted out being shot. People in the audience started gesturing and shouting. Kiefer didn't know what was happening, and by the time he did, the demonstrators were all sitting down. Kiefer muttered something about kids being kids, and that was it."

"That was it?" Simpson asked.

"That was it." I threw out my arms.

"And you had nothing to do with it."

"Why should I?" I raised my voice a little.

"Maybe something with your dad?"

I was getting mad. "My dad hasn't demonstrated for years. Besides he'd never get involved with a graduation. He's got better things to do." I could imagine some teachers asking me this, but not Simpson.

He waited for a second and then went on. "There's going to be an investigation of the incident, and you're going to be called in."

I guess I could have been grateful that he warned me, but I wasn't grateful. I was just plain pissed. "This is bullshit," I said. "Complete bullshit. Those morons are smart enough to know my dad wouldn't do this. And they know I wouldn't. I was a junior. I'll tell them what I know, which is nothing, and then tell them to get fucked." A couple of half-asleep old guys slouched at a table next to ours looked over approvingly.

Simpson held out his hands to get me to lower my voice. "Tell them what you know. That should be enough." Then he smiled in a pained kind of way. "Max, they're investigating me, too."

"Why you?" This was getting weird.

"They're covering all the bases. Several of the graduates with signs were my students. The school folks just might ask you what you and I have talked about. They'll know we chat a lot in the hall. They might ask kind of innocently if we ever discussed your dad." Then he really paused and swallowed hard. "You don't need to tell them that I told you how much I admired him. In fact, I'd appreciate it if you didn't mention that."

I shrugged. "I can do that. But would it really matter if I told the whole truth?"

He wasn't enjoying this, but he kept talking. "I've told my classes how much I hate what we've done in the Middle East. I said if I had been around in the '60s I would have been a protestor. My wife and I thought they might just put this all together and dump me. I don't have tenure. I'm still temporary here. It would be no trouble getting rid of me." He kept running his hands through his hair and twisting his neck. I looked away.

"This is Mrs. Simpson's idea?"

"Our idea. I've got a family. I like this job. This is important." He was blinking and fiddling with the salt shaker.

I couldn't sit in this crappy place any longer. I couldn't talk to this guy any longer. I'd lie for him, but I wouldn't stay any longer. I stood up and shook his hand. I told him that I would say we never talked about the protest or about my dad. I'd tell them that he would never want to disrupt something important like a graduation.

Then I walked out and got on my bike and took the long way to my job at Casey's Stationery Store. I passed a warehouse that used to be full of clothes. One time my dad and I had climbed over the fence and sneaked inside and walked around.

At Casey's, I unpacked stuff for a few hours and then told Casey I had a stomach ache and went home.

When I got home, I found my dad in the backyard. He was wearing shorts and a tie-dyed T-shirt and sitting at a table writing something on his laptop—probably a letter to a Congressman. He looked over at me and said my mom had called to say she was having dinner with a potential funder. "It looks like pizza for the guys."

A few hours later we were sitting at a booth at Dominick's, and I was telling him about Simpson. I didn't expect my dad to do anything, and I didn't want him to, I guess. He had already told me several times that the graduation demonstration was silly, but still amusing. He said that again. He said Simpson sounded like 'a bit of a weenie,' but these days with all the security, he might have been right to worry. That was it. That was a big conversation for us.

As it turned out, I was never called in. I don't know if Simpson had been called in, but if he had, it must not have mattered because he was back teaching at the school in the fall. He was good, as I knew he would be, but I didn't participate much, and he knew why. No more joking in the hallway.

Later that September I was in the den watching a ball game on TV, and my dad came into the room. He turned off the set and sat next to me on the couch. This was not the kind of thing he did. He told me he had been thinking about the Simpson business. "What's interesting, Max, is the power you had at that moment. You could have gone to the school, told the truth about Simpson, maybe exaggerated a little, left out some things, and I bet they would have fired the guy. Ended his career. Ruined his life. As a protestor and a letter writer, I've never had much power. I don't even have the power to get your mom to stop seeing Dr. Fowler." He didn't look hurt or angry. It was all matter-of-fact.

He got up and turned on the game. The Cubs were losing. Then he looked back at me on the couch in my sweatshirt and shorts and with my abandoned homework assignments. He stopped by the door and turned. From that angle I couldn't see his ponytail. "See you in the morning, buddy. I love you."

"I love you too, Dad."

Coach

I could never make up my mind if Mr. Miles Manning looked old or young. Up close you could see the wrinkles and spots on his hands and face. And loose skin hung from his neck. And he had dark marks under his eyes. But from across the field he looked like a young guy with red hair. And he acted young, too, because he was really kind of simple. He was probably the simplest adult I had ever met. Not retarded—just simple. Whatever happened, he'd just smile and shrug.

People at Forest High called him 'Coach' even though he had coached only one year as assistant for the sophomore football team, and that was ten years ago. My brother was on that team and said Manning didn't know the difference between a field goal and a fair catch. Most of the time he'd walk around with that dopey smile on his face saying things like, "Go get 'em, guys. Go get 'em." In one game he actually cheered when the other team scored a touchdown. When that happened, even the cheerleaders froze. Instead of apologizing or making up an excuse, he just shrugged. My brother said it was like it didn't matter to him, or if it did, he couldn't do anything. I heard that was the last day he ever coached at Forest High.

But everyone still called him 'Coach,' even though he was nothing more than a P.E. flunky. His job title was some kind of assistant. Before class, he took roll. When we had swimming, he passed out towels. When we played touch football, he moved the yard-line markers. If the teacher in charge forgot something, Coach would hustle back to get it. "Manning, I forgot the bases. Run back and get them, okay?"

"Go, Coach," we'd all shout and off he'd sprint. He loved
to run. Most of the time he would take the long way around.
A few minutes later, we'd see him tearing towards us with his
arms full of bases, and we'd give another big cheer.

But even though he seemed really stupid when he sprinted
across the field, he looked happy and relaxed. I'd call it *easy*—
everything about Coach was easy. He was supposed to be a
smart guy. He came to Forest as a history teacher. My brother
said he knew a lot about Lincoln and the people you study in
American history. One time he brought in a World War II hand
grenade. Another time he brought in a letter written by Teddy
Roosevelt. He also wrote articles for some teacher magazine.
But he couldn't make the kids shut up. I guess they didn't want
to fire him, so they reassigned him to the P.E. department. Right
after they took away his job, my brother saw him alone in his
old classroom. The lights were out, and he had all of his teaching stuff on his desk, and he was staring out the window.

But he was an odd dude. Last year he caught up with me as we
were walking back to the locker room across the football field.

"Archie, I've got to ask you something," he said. He had noticed
I was wearing a shirt with a picture of the blues singer Koko
Taylor. That really excited him. He told me that two summers
ago he had dropped off his wife with her family in Indiana and
driven all by himself through the Mississippi Delta where a
lot of those old blues singers had lived. He knew what to look
for because he had read a book about the old singers. He even
played blues music in the car. He asked me if I loved the blues
as much as he did. I said I didn't know anything about music
and that the shirt belonged to my brother. Coach frowned, but
then he gave me a big nod and a smile, and I smiled back. From
that time on, he made a point of calling me 'Koko.'

When you got to be an upperclassman at Forest, you got to make fun of Coach. You couldn't do it as a freshman, but by the time you were a junior, it was cool. People copied the way he stood with his hands on his hips and rolled his head, looking up at the sky where there was nothing to see. They spoke in his high, scratchy voice. They threw a ball the way he did—just like a girl. Rick Babson was the best impersonator by far. Rick was this big, blond kid on his way to Yale, and even though he didn't look like Coach, he could still do a perfect imitation. He'd drop his shoulders and walk with his feet out. He would gesture in a big, silly kind of way. We'd crack up every time.

Coach must have known what was going on. Some guys would actually speak in his voice when he was nearby. And during games, people would break off into Manning runs. Even the coaches. Sometimes, when it got really bad, he would make his stupid smile even bigger and go off to fiddle with a base or check the pressure of the soccer balls, just to look busy. Mostly he acted like he got it, that everyone was laughing *with* him and not *at* him.

I could copy him, too, but I wasn't very good at making fun of people. And, to tell you the truth, it was hard to make fun of him because I knew he liked me. This was obvious ever since he told me about the blues. He didn't say much, but I would catch him looking at me. Once in a touch football game, he listened in on the other team's huddle and then nodded at the guy who was going to catch the pass. When I made the interception on the next play, Coach clapped and everyone hooted. It gave me a really creepy feeling inside. Another time he stopped me in the hall to tell me that when he retired in two years, his wife said he could study music in the city.

"I think he's queer for you, Archie," Weldon shouted one day driving home. He had to shout because the muffler of his van

was shot. "He's always looking at you. You'd better be careful
in the shower." We were driving near the projects. Weldon went
this way when he wanted to buy weed. He didn't tell me that's
why he stopped at the old apartment and went inside, but I knew.

I wasn't considered a real pot smoker, so supposedly I didn't
know how things worked. If someone brought out a joint at a
party, I might take a hit, but that was it. I wasn't into the whole
business of buying and selling. And it wasn't that big a deal, anyway. We were just kids going off to college and having a little
fun our senior year.

Actually, I wasn't going off to college because I would be
staying home to run the family restaurant, Dominick's. My dad
dropped dead when I was a freshman, and I was the one to keep
the place going because my brother and his family lived in California. We all thought it would be great if I worked during the
day and went to community college at night. That was fine with
me. I wouldn't have been going to a good college anyway.

I was a good fit for the restaurant. My hair was starting to recede
a little bit, and I had started to call adults by their first names.
Rudy the barber had even asked me to join a bowling league.

One time Coach and his wife came into the restaurant. I
looked up from my *Sports Illustrated* and saw Mrs. Manning heading for a table in the back with Coach following along. It was the
kind of place where people just walked in and sat down at one
of the tables or at the counter. The table where they sat had no
window, but there was a large poster of the Italian Alps. Coach
read the menu, and she sat there with her head slightly bowed.
She was small like the Coach, but she looked firm. Whenever
I saw her around town, she was always wearing plain colors and
had her hair pulled back like a pioneer woman. My mom said
that Mrs. Manning worked in a hospital in the city and that she
had grown up in a religious community in Indiana.

The Coach had a cheeseburger, and Mrs. Manning ordered a garden salad. During the meal he took out a map and leaned it against the napkin holder so that they both could see it. After they finished eating, they were standing by the counter. She had just paid the bill, and he had been standing off to the side looking at a picture of the restaurant that had been taken twenty years ago. "Frieda," he suddenly spoke up, "this young man is Archie Ori. He's a senior at the high school."

Mrs. Manning stopped fussing with her change purse and looked right at me. "Hello, Archie." She spoke clearly. "And whom are you named after?" She tipped her head and stared into my face. From that angle, I could see that she wasn't wearing earrings.

It was an odd question, but I tried to answer it. "My grand-father was named Archibald, so I guess that's why. He came here from Italy."

"And whom was he named after? Archie is an unusual name for Italians." For a second I thought she was going to take notes. When I told her I didn't know, she frowned. Then she smiled and reached over the counter to shake my hand. "Nice to meet you, Archie Ori. Whoever you are. Come on, Miles. We have to do more weeding before it gets dark." Out the door she marched with Coach hustling to keep up. But he did look back at me with one of his simple smiles. And naturally he shrugged.

They lived in a small house about two blocks away. It backed up on a huge field where people grew vegetables. Mrs. Manning could walk everywhere from there. And she would catch the train to the hospital. As I watched them leave, I wondered if she had any idea how often the kids made fun of her husband.

The Hartmut Incident happened in the spring, a few weeks before graduation. We had this exchange student from Dusseldorf named Hartmut Wuhlrob, and he was a complete dork.

In fact, we made fun of him as much as we made fun of Coach, and I would join in, too. He would say things like 'waycation,' when he meant 'vacation,' and he wore his pants too high. And he could never quite figure out what we were talking about.

But he did figure out that we liked to make fun of Coach. One day we were lying down between halves of a soccer game when all of a sudden, this goofy German leaped up and crouched over us and started chattering in what he must have thought was a Manning voice. And he did all of this right in front of Coach. And when Coach tried to get away, Hartmut actually chased him and kept on jabbering. It was sickening.

Well, Babson went nuts. That wasn't the way we did things. He walked up to Hartmut and shoved him down right beside a soccer goal. "If you do that any more, you fucking kraut, I'll punch your pig eyes into your skull." Hartmut lay on the ground stammering in German. We were in a semicircle, hoping that they would fight. And off to the side with his mouth opening and closing stood Coach. For just a second I thought he was going to say something, but instead he stared at his hands and kept moving his lips.

Then he turned and tore across the fields right through the middle of a freshman soccer game, into the parking lot and headed towards his house. Some students standing next to a car smoking leaped out of the way when they saw him coming. They said his face was wild, not like it usually was at all.

Coach didn't come to school those last two weeks before everything closed down for the summer. I didn't see him in the hall. Someone said he had called in sick. Someone else said they heard shouting from his house.

We had a small party in the restaurant the day after graduation. My mom let the kids drink if they promised to walk home. She also stayed in the front of the restaurant so she didn't have to catch anyone smoking pot in the back alley. We did adult things like shaking hands and hugging. My friends wished me good luck with my job and community college. I'm sure they didn't believe me when I said I was glad that I was staying home. Towards the end of the evening Babson staggered in with an older girl. He had lipstick on his face. The girl's blouse was buttoned wrong. He was loaded but still sharp enough to do one of his best Coach impersonations. Then someone suggested we call Coach, but I vetoed that idea. Someone else said they had seen him in town and that he looked like an old man. "He didn't even have that dumb smile. He just walked right by me like a zombie." And he was always alone—in the summer his wife visited her family in Indiana.

When he did come into the restaurant that summer, he barely said hello. Strangers must have thought he was some kind of street person because his shirt wasn't tucked in and he needed a shave. He'd shuffle in and head for a table in the back. He'd have a book, but instead of reading it, he would just stare at the table top. Once I walked over to his table and tried to start a conversation about black singers, but he just nodded. "When does Mrs. Manning get back from Indiana?" I asked before I walked back to my place behind the counter.

"It's hard to say." He didn't look up. "Her sisters need her down there to help with the farm." He wasn't going to say anything more. Man, he looked sad. I thought that she had to be pretty mean to leave him like this.

I played catcher on a softball team that summer. In the second game I hit a home run. When I crossed home plate, I saw Coach in the crowd, but he wasn't cheering. I also signed up for my community college courses. At the time I thought for a second about asking Coach for advice in picking out classes. But then I could see how lame that would look.

I also spent more time with my mom. Now that I was an adult, it was okay to do things like that. We would sit in the living room of our apartment with the TV on. She always sat in the same chair where she could see the picture of my brother with the other members of the National Honor Society. There was also a picture of my father accepting the Class B golf championship trophy at the local course. Like lots of golfers, he was a short and stocky guy. When that picture was taken, he hadn't told any of us that he had a bad heart. Maybe he didn't know. Mom still wore her wedding ring, but she had to get it fixed to fit her skinny fingers because she had lost a lot of weight since he died. All she really wanted to talk about was the restaurant. Should we hire a new cook? What about expanding? Would it be a good idea for me to take some restaurant management courses in college? These were probably the same things she said to my dad when he was alive. I didn't ask what she thought about all those times she was alone.

Towards the end of July, I saw Coach gardening. He was on his knees weeding in this place he had cleared out. It looked like he planned to plant something. He and Mrs. Manning were supposed to have a spectacular garden, but it looked a little sickly to me, especially with that big bare spot.

"How are you doing, Coach?" I called out and walked over to him. He stood up and shook my hand.

"Nice to see you, Archie." He actually smiled a little. "How's business at your restaurant?" He was wearing a baggy blue jogging suit that was big enough for Babson.

"Business is great. We had to hire a new dishwasher. Next year the Rotary Club will start meeting at our place." I was really glad to see him.

"That's got to make you and your mom happy." He started to smile a little bit more.

"You know it does. I've also started doing some of the cooking." I felt like talking, and he seemed kind of interested, so I told him that my brother was coming to town in a month.

"I knew him. Isn't his name Dominick, just like your Dad? He's the one who gave you the Koko Taylor shirt." This was the first time I had seen that stupid grin for quite a while. And it made me feel good. I had forgotten what it was like to be around the Coach. "When he was on the sophomore football team, I was one of the assistants. You must have heard that I cheered for the other team one time." He looked off in the distance towards the school. From where we were standing you could see the smokestack and part of the field. I could even see the place by the soccer goal where Babson had threatened to punch out Hartmut's eyes.

"When he gets to town, I'll let you know. I know he'd like to see you. When you come to the restaurant, we can all talk." I felt myself slipping into an adult voice. This was the kind of things adults did—making plans to get together.

But he wasn't really listening anymore. He had gone back to his knees and was pulling out weeds. "Maybe so, Archie." His voice was faint and hard to understand. "Maybe so. But I might be gone. I have two more weeks to decide if I'm coming back."

"Coach, you can't retire!"

"I can still take early retirement. It might be time for me to do some more traveling." He had found a way to turn his back on me. He had stopped pulling at the ground. I didn't really want to see the expression on his face.

"I have lots of work here," he said. And then, just before I started walking back to town, he looked right at me and said, "Archie, you're a lucky man." I stood there and then walked off.

My brother came and went. We drove to a Cubs game in the city. I bicycled with his kids over to the high school so they could see where their father had been an athlete and an honor student.

My brother's wife helped in the kitchen. She even prepared one
of the specials: 'Anne's Mighty Meatloaf.' On their last day, she
took my mother to the mall and bought her three new outfits.
Up until this trip, I had called her 'my brother's wife.' Now
I called her my 'sister-in-law.' And then they flew back to San
Diego. I hadn't even mentioned Coach.

    Then late that August I stopped by Coach's house. He didn't
answer after I rang the doorbell, but I could hear him shuffling
inside, so I didn't go anywhere. Finally he opened the door about
a foot and peered out. He blinked. His skin was white, and his
eyes were pink. He looked really old. He was wearing the same
jogging suit that he wore gardening, but it looked even bigger.
His hair hadn't been cut. I could see some gray in the corners.
It had never occurred to me that maybe he dyed it red.

    "Archie? What are you doing here?"

    "Can I come in?" I had never been inside his house. We all
imagined it to be plain and clean, just like his wife. It wouldn't
have trophies or family pictures. Before today, I hadn't wanted
to see it because it might show me what a depressing guy Coach
really was.

    "Not today, Archie." His voice was flat and dry. "The house is
a mess. I'm packing up." I got this feeling if I tried to barge in,
he would block the way.

    "It's time to go then?" My voice sounded low and far away.

    "Oh, yes. It's time to go." He opened the door a little wider, but
not much. "I told the principal I wanted early retirement. Schools
love that, you know. Now they can hire some new teacher for
much less money. I didn't do anything, anyway." His feet were
fidgeting. He smelled different, odd. Like an old man, I guess.
I had never seen such an unhappy looking human being.

    "That day Babson got so mad at the German. That did it,
didn't it? That was the day you decided not to come back?"

"That was a bad day. The worst. But I've had some bad days. You have no idea." I could still picture him with that stunned expression looking over at Babson and the German.

"How does Mrs. Manning feel about your retiring? Did you get in touch with her in Indiana?"

"She's not coming back, Archie. I sent her away." He cleared his throat and leaned against the door.

"Will you see her again?" Any kids pedaling by on their bikes or people walking with their dogs would have no idea what was happening on the front porch of this little man's house.

"I'll stop and see her in Indiana. She'll show me the church where she works. Then I'll drive south and look for a job." He stood up straighter. He wanted me to leave.

My hands were tingling. Sweat was starting to sneak down my arm. Finally I shook his hand and put my arm around him. Man, did he have bony shoulders.

Special Project

"A plan, Clemons? Do you have a plan? A strategy? An escape?
A way to cover your ass?"

Arthur Clemons could hear the impatience and weariness in
Jim's voice. Thursday was not Jim's usual drinking night. But Jim
went on. "Can you make it look like you didn't forget the kid
was in your class? Jesus. If Mildred was still around, this wouldn't
have happened."

At 11:30 PM on a school night, Kelly's Tap was practically empty.
Kelly was slouched in the corner reading *The Racing Form*. Next
to him a silent TV set was showing an ancient rerun of MASH. Customers walked behind the bar to pour a beer and leave the money
beside the cash register. Jim and Clemons sat at the bar. To their
left was an old couple whispering intently at each other.

"Yeah, I've got a plan—if you want to call it that. It's all I have
left." Clemons frowned at a full glass of beer in front of him
and wondered if he would ever want to drink again. "First, I
find Jerome. It won't be easy because the little scumbag is swimming around with the other lowlifes of Forest High. I'll tell him
that he's still in my class, but to make it official, he'll have to
come back. His work out of class will count as a special project."
Clemons could almost feel the disbelieving stare of his friend.
Jim, they both knew, could fuck up almost as badly as Clemons
could, but Jim would always catch himself in time. He would
never lose track of a student.

"I'll even make sure," Clemons continued, "that my record
book shows he's written most of the papers and taken the tests.
And then I'll even give him a grade." He sighed and winced and

looked with more interest at the beer. He pushed back his mop of curly black hair and scowled at his hands.

"So," Jim yawned, "your plan is to lie." He reached over the bar to draw himself a beer.

"Lie through my teeth. I'll manufacture the past. Call it 'creative nonfiction.'" He made quotation marks with his fingers.

"Tell the truth," Jim said flatly. "Tell that moron Morton the simple truth."

"The truth? Are you nuts? Are you fucking nuts?" The couple down the bar stopped whispering and looked in Clemons' direction. "You want me to admit that I forgot this kid was in my class, that somehow I left his name out of the grade book. For eight weeks he's been humping fourteen-year-olds and selling Ecstasy while his classmates have been comparing Brutus and Cassius." He reached into his side pocket for a cigarette pack. It was empty. He leaned over the bar and grabbed one from a pack left by Kelly.

"When Morton confronted you with this, what did you say?"

"Vice Principal Morton tracked me down during a free period. He asked me to come to his office. I thought it might still be something about that disturbance in the library. He was still pissed that I gave students the key to the building. But then, from out of nowhere, he curled his snout, grunted, and matter-of-factly inquired about Jerome Simmons."

"And you practically shit." Jim broke out in a half smile.

"Did I ever. It all came back. At one time, I had known the little viper was probably in the class, but I figured he had dropped. I meant to do something, but I never got around to it. Then I totally forgot and time went by and here I am sitting in this asshole's office and grades—freakin' grades—are due next week. Un-fucking-believable." Clemons reached for his beer, stared hard at the foam and drained the whole glass. He stood up and walked to the back, held the empty glass under the spigot and pulled the tap.

"Didn't he ask to see your grade book? I can see his great brow furrowing and his lips moving as he tries to make sense of your handwriting."

"I told him the grade book was back at my apartment. I frowned a lot and raised my eyebrows when he told me that Jerome had been spotted out of class when he should have been in English with me. Most of the time he spent asking me how a kid who was supposed to be studying English could be unaccounted for. He's almost positive that I forgot about Jerome. He just wants to act professionally. He doesn't want to make a big deal because it will take time away from coaching defensive ends. I told him that Jerome had been in class, but that he—along with a lot of seniors—was working on special projects."

"Artie, old buddy, your plan sucks. You can't trust that Simmons kid to go along with you. He wears a nipple ring. Make a new plan."

"It's too late."

"Why not say you forgot? What can they do?"

"Plenty. Fuckin' plenty. Last year I got in all that shit for borrowing money from my students. The administration's always sending me notes about smoking in the building. And then I let Ferguson drive the school van."

"You let a student..."

"Don't *you* give me any shit. Besides, I had no choice. I got in more trouble because the literary magazine went $2,500 over budget and I caught serious grief for Audrey Rogers' poem."

"'Ode to Fellatio'?"

"It turned out to be a sonnet. I lose this job and I'm finished as a teacher. Believe me." Clemons glared defiantly back at his reflection in the mirror behind the bar. That morning in the bathroom mirror he had seen a living corpse—haggard and exhausted. A recently released hostage. Now, after talking to his best friend and coming up with an escape plan, he looked partially alive. Maybe the alcohol was boosting his confidence, but his color was back and he was sitting straight. "Jim, old buddy, they might call you in on this. You teach right next to me. We've been colleagues for years."

"If they call me in," Jim sighed, "I'll remind them that you're a gifted teacher, but a little careless. I'll tell them you're popular with the 'troubled' students. I'll list all of your accomplishments. And then I'll assure them that Jerome was part of an independent project. But, Artie," Jim threw back his head, "this is the last time. I have a family and a future. Find some other hobby, for Christ's sake."

Clemons tracked down Jerome during the lunch period. He was leaning against his red Chevy in the parking lot, smoking a long, thin cigar. He was wearing a red kerchief as a headband and holding a cell phone. He was a short, solid kid who had once wrestled, but that was way back when he was a freshman. Since then he'd aimed his life away from the mat. Everyone, including Clemons, assumed that he used drugs and sold them. Beyond that who knew? He wore lots of leather and stood close to his girl friends. And there were plenty of these—libidinous, foulmouthed, chain-smoking little nymphets that all looked the same to Clemons. Girls who would yawn right in his face.

"Jerome, we have to talk." He tried to look tall. Jerome's smile grew to expose a front tooth sporting a red jewel of some kind.

He lifted the phone and began to punch numbers. "Coral, I'll be a little late. This time bring everything with you." He hung up and put the phone next to a briefcase on the top of his car. Even in his unease, Clemons could recognize that it was exactly like the briefcase his department chairman had recently lost.

"Mr. Clemons," Jerome said gleefully, "What are you doing in our parking lot? The last time I saw you, you were writing a check to Audrey Rogers. Something about a car payment."

Clemons had no time for small talk. "Jerome..." He moved slightly closer, turning his back on a group of smokers standing close by. He selected his serious teacher voice. "Jerome, we need to talk. You are still a student in my senior English class. I forgot to write your name in the book, but as far as the school is concerned, you are in there earning credits. That was eight weeks ago. I have to give you a grade." He wanted this to be fast and serious. "For your sake, I can't tell the administration that you were cutting."

"For my sake?" Jerome's eyes widened as they came more into focus.

"All right, for our sakes. Look, this can be done easily. If Vice Principal Morton asks, say you've been in class, but from time to time you worked on special projects away from the classroom."

"No problemo, Artie. I did use that time for all kinds of special projects. Some of them even took me into Chicago."

Right then Clemons became aware of a girl sprawled in the back scat of the Chevy. Everything but her purple hair and face was covered by an enormous tie-dyed T-shirt. She wore a nose ring and an eyebrow ringlet. Could she be naked? Could she be dead?

"Don't worry about Mimi. She's just taking a nap. We had a late study date last night."

Clemons nodded and went back to business. "Anyway, you come back; I'll let you make up some of the work, and then I can give you a grade."

"What did I get?"

"How about a c?"

"A c! Come on, Clemons. I'm not coming back for a c. I've got too much to lose...give me a B+ and I'll stop around."

"You'll have to do some work, most of the work. Do you have your books?"

"In the trunk." He grabbed the briefcase and phone from the roof of his car. Clemons followed Jerome to the back of the Chevy and watched him open the trunk. It was, he had to admit, a fantastic thing to behold. The school books were in a bag from the bookstore. The receipts were probably still in them. Other bags, stereo equipment, two laptop computers, several brown packages, sleeping bags, and a case of Two Fingers Tequila filled the rest of the space.

"I've got a meeting now, Artie. See you on Monday." Checking his watch, Jerome tossed the briefcase into the trunk and slammed it closed, then moved quickly to the driver's door and climbed in. Before he sped away, he shook Clemons' hand as he gave him a large smile and a wink.

"Make sure you bring your copy of *Julius Caesar* and a notebook," Clemons shouted feebly at the disappearing car. Only the smokers heard this plea.

Clemons planned a video for Jerome's return—a full period film entitled *What Happens in Julius Caesar*. It was a 'content rich' educational film made by the Illinois Humanities Council. Jerome would sit near the front. Some kids might think he had been there the whole time. The rest wouldn't care. Only Tina Jones, an honor student and active in community service, would figure out what was happening. Tina could be trouble if the plan didn't work to perfection. After the class, Clemons would give a few special assignments. One of these would go to Jerome.

He also pinned up new pieces of student writing on the bulletin boards. He even considered poetry by Audrey Rogers, but nothing seemed suitable. He did find a sample of Jerome's writing from last year. A description of a jazz bar.

To Clemons' delight, Jerome marched in early. He even
dropped a folder on Clemons' desk. The words SPECIAL PROJECT
were emblazoned on the front. Clemons felt a vague unease but
nodded casually and gestured to the seat near the front. "We'll
have to make an appointment to discuss your independent
projects."

Jerome nodded importantly and reached for his notebook.
Clemons felt like applauding. The night before he had fixed
the grade book. By a stroke of luck Chloe Stone had dropped
the class in September. This gave Clemons a spot for Jerome in
the right part of the alphabet. For several of the days he wrote
down I.P. for independent project. He made sure the ink color
always matched. He was pleased with his work.

The class filled. Clemons made a short announcement as he
turned down the lights and turned on the DVD. "As you've heard
me say before, I want you to hear a more traditional explanation
of *Julius Caesar.* The narrator will explain the theory of tragedy
and then show how it works in the play. He uses actors—bad
ones. But he knows what he's talking about. When the movie
is over, I'll have you write about it and report back tomorrow.
I want to know if you learned anything." By now the film had
started and an old guy with a pipe and leather elbow patches was
speaking earnestly into the camera. Jerome, who had listened
carefully to Clemons' introduction, now looked bored. *Don't
you dare go to sleep, you little fucker,* Clemons said to himself. *Keep
those beady little eyes open.*

About fifteen minutes into the movie, it happened. The
actors had just completed the scene with Brutus and Calpurnia.
The professor was explaining for the eighth time that Brutus'
character was leading him down a tragic path. Some of the kids
had laughed at the bad costumes, but most seemed to be paying
attention. Tina Jones was taking lots of notes. She had moved

to a desk closer to the screen. Even Jerome looked alert. And
once he even scribbled something down in his notebook. Then,
just as Caesar was about to enter the Senate, Jerome's phone
rang, an obnoxious series of beeps. Clemons could the beeps
pulsing in his stomach lining.

It shouldn't have mattered. These things happen all the
time. A good teacher learns to deal with such interruptions.
Ordinarily the class would turn and laugh. The teacher might
have to say, "All right, class, let's get back to our film." But this
was different because instead of turning off the phone and
apologizing, Jerome leaped to his feet and jogged toward the
door. He muttered something to Clemons on his way out and
then was gone, leaving a few beeps behind.

Clemons tore after him, but all he could see was the back
of the leather jacket at the far end of the corridor. Clemons re-
entered the classroom, seized his grade book, turned furiously to
the current page, and slashed an absence mark next to Jerome's
name. Like those of the actors in the movie, his gestures were
big and obvious. He was glad the lights were out so he didn't
have to see Tina Jones' expression. On the screen Marc Antony
was delivering his funeral oration, but by now most of the kids
were in deep conversation. Clemons sat dazed at his desk and
let them talk. The DVD ended; the bell rang. He was alone.

He looked down at his hands. They were yellow with nicotine.
The nails were chewed to the nub. Next to them lay Jerome's
SPECIAL PROJECT folder. Clemons reached for the package,
opened it, and poured out the contents. No compositions but
lots of stuff: several condom packages, cigarette paper, a small
spoon, and a CD. The CD was neatly labeled A PARKING LOT CHAT
WITH MR. CLEMONS. OCTOBER 28, 2010. Under these words was
one more, a word that surely Jerome did not have to write. But
he did anyway. The word was COPY.

Funny in the Summer

Armand looked up from his book as a rangy blond girl with a red headband strode into the empty teachers' cafeteria. She swept past the table where, during the year, bridge players hung out, and came right up to where he was sitting by himself at a corner table. "I'm Julie Perkins," she held out her hand. "The new English teacher slash assistant basketball coach. I sat right behind you at the meeting this morning. And you're?"

Armand looked up, shook her hand, and mumbled his name. He remembered the young person at the summer school faculty meeting.

She sat down across from him, pulled a water bottle from her bag, and kept right on talking. "What's it like teaching summer school?"

Armand blinked and sat up straight. "Don't ask me. I've never taught summer school before. I suppose the place will feel empty. When I'm here during the year, it's crawling with kids." He thought about the halls of Forest High School clogged with jabbering young people. He kept his voice neutral. No reason to be rude, but he felt no interest in bantering.

"Never been here in the summer!" *Or any other time,* Armand thought. Julie reached over and patted his hand. "Home alone!" she laughed. "You can hang out in the auto shop or practice kicking field goals outside."

Armand smiled but not much. "Or I could put on one-man plays in the drama department or snooze in one of the buses or I could take the bus for a spin." He paused. "Actually, I wouldn't be here this summer at all except that Jimmy Sanders inherited a cleaning business and moved back to Peoria. I'm doing the

English department a favor." Even though he found himself talking, Armand was still not used to people coming over to his table, much less touching him. During the year, with bridge players and other faculty people filling the tables, he might have politely let this newcomer know he didn't want company.

For decades he had graded papers at this table by himself. He had plenty of time to be with others at faculty parties and on the golf course, but in the cafeteria he never did much talking.

"Well then, it must really feel different?" the girl continued. "It's got to feel creepy with the building so empty. Kind of odd." Julie was chewing gum, and she raised her eyebrows when she spoke and looked right into his eyes.

"Little things will be odd, I guess," Armand said. "Like teaching in shorts. I'm not sure what the kids will have to say about my knees. But I guess they should see them before I retire."

She stopped chewing her gum and stared at him. "You're not thinking of packing it in, are you?"

"Not for a few years. But I am in my sixties." He couldn't believe he was having this conversation with a stranger.

"And then what? An old folks' reservation?"

He shook his head and told her he planned to read and to garden. He had an offer from a local publisher to work on a textbook project. In the summer he'd play golf. In the winter he'd travel. Plus he could do some consulting for the school district. "Actually, I'm looking forward to my retirement. I know how to fill up my time."

"That sounds great, Armand." Now she was calling him by his first name. "Just be sure you do it. Don't quit. We had a neighbor in Ohio who sat so long in front of the TV set after he retired that he had to have his legs amputated. Can you imagine that? They chopped off his legs because he didn't use them. You don't ever want to quit."

It was dumbfounding that this person could talk so matter-of-factly about quitting. Did she know that only two weeks ago he had been named Forest's 'Teacher of the Decade'? At the end-of-the-year party, the superintendent had presented Armand with a plaque and then proclaimed, "Most of us start shrinking, but this guy keeps growing." Not one teacher who watched him tearfully accept the award would ever think of him as a quitter.

Armand cleared his throat and looked around the empty room. During the school year the cafeteria smelled like soup and hot dogs. Now it smelled more like wax. The sound of the milk machine from across the room reached his ears. He turned back and noticed how athletic Julie looked—short, blond hair, boyish face, erect posture, and the gum. When the assistant principal introduced her at the morning meeting, he said that she had coached jv basketball at Lehigh.

"What are you doing at Forest?" Armand suddenly asked. Was he being polite? Curious? He wasn't sure.

She tipped her chair back and started to talk. Thirteen years before, she had been about to start teaching, but then Bud came along and she married him. "He knew all about software—how to make it, use it, and improve it. Bill Gates wanted to hire him. Bud wanted me to have time for business trips, so I turned down my first teaching job. He was so serious and alert that I couldn't resist him. A very serious guy."

They traveled to Abu Dhabi, Bangladesh, Bolivia, Andorra, Manchuria, and Bhutan. They even spent a month in Albania. They traveled so much that they never had a family or a place to live. Then one day outside of an inn in the Cotswolds, she found Bud slumped over the steering wheel of their rented Land Rover. A massive heart attack. "I loved him, Armand, but he was exhausting. Too smart. Too much energy. It was horrible to see a guy with so much future sprawled out dead." *Sprawled out?* Armand wondered if she had carried him from the car before she called the British police.

Fifteen minutes into this conversation and she had told him all of this. A few minutes later she started in on him. "Are you married?"

"Not anymore. I was married once to a vice president of a downtown bank." He paused. He could hear the drone of the floor-waxing machine. The sound carried in the empty building. "We didn't like each other." That was all he needed to tell her.

"Did splitting up make you sad?" Julie reached down to re-tie her jogging shoes. She was still chewing gum. But she kept her eyes on him.

"Not really. It was going to happen." Actually he had been relieved to tear loose from Audrey, who had come to consider him a total loser. Sometimes at night, when he was grading papers, he would hear fierce breathing behind him. He would turn and find a scowling Audrey shaking her head. She would usually mutter something and stalk back to watch TV in the bedroom. Audrey had no idea how much he loved writing his precise, helpful comments on student themes. She could not imagine how good it felt to return them promptly. This was how it had to be done. Then one night, Audrey poured a pot of black coffee into his briefcase, drenching a batch of senior term papers. The next day they both called lawyers. Instead of telling Julie all of this, he simply added, "It was a good thing, a very good thing for both of us." After Audrey, he had dated an American History teacher. They had gone to plays and movies together. Occasionally she'd spend the night. She was retired now in North Carolina, and Armand figured maybe he'd see her from time to time after he retired.

Julie changed the subject. "What are you teaching this summer?"

He told her he planned for his students to write several long personal narratives and to read *Catcher in the Rye, The Great Gatsby, Billy Budd,* and other novels. "It's American Literature, and I can do pretty much what I want."

"Are you as good an English teacher as they say?" She stared hard at him.

"They?"

"The other teachers and the principal."

"Yes. I am." He leaned over and grabbed his old leather brief-case but remained sitting. "I've got to meet a friend for dinner."

"I'm going to play softball. See you tomorrow, Armand. Your room is next to mine." He thought about walking out with her, but instead he stayed seated and watched her march through the room and out the door. "See ya," she called back.

The next day classes started, and Armand arrived early at his windowless classroom, which was used during the regular year by coaches who taught health and drivers' education. The walls were bare except for a poster of Peyton Manning, whose teeth had been turned into Dracula fangs. On the door was a poster of an AIDS victim—an emaciated black child with bulging eyes. The caption read, CONDOM SENSE. On the wall was also an old photo of Forest High. It had been taken early in the century. Armand was studying it when the door opened and in walked Julie in blue shorts and an orange Hawaiian shirt. "You know, Armand," she laughed, pointing at his shorts, "you might be right about those knees."

Now that they were both standing, he could see that Julie was a little taller than he was, but not much. "Back to teacher pants tomorrow?" he asked.

"Might be a good idea. It's all about dignity."

"No gum today?"

"Not with the kids."

He cleared his throat. "Ready to teach?" It was the right thing to say, but he was curious to see how far her confidence went.

"I'm ready, Coach. I'm ready to get some freshmen prepared for the rigors of English. They'll write about what they 'know' and what they 'should know.' They'll read short stories and take a few trips." With that she held up a fist, waited until he hand-bumped her, and left to teach.

After class she joined him in the cafeteria. "I'm going to like it here," she smiled. "One of my kids wrote about his uncle's tattoo parlor."

"Any discipline problems?"

"Nope. After all, I am a coach, and I've been around the world," she laughed. "These are just little suburban weenies. And anyway the summer makes them mellow."

Armand told her about his first class. "We read a Poe story and talked about it. Before that, we talked about what goes into a good story. Then we shared some stories."

"Any good ones?"

"A girl named Cindy described waking up her grandmother. She didn't know that old lady kept her false teeth in a glass next to her bed. Cindy screamed and ran out of the room."

"Did you laugh?"

"We all laughed."

"Armand," Julie lowered her voice. "You are a funny guy. You look like a regular old school teacher with your gray hair and glasses, but I think you are really a funny guy. Am I right?"

Her question surprised him and made him feel a little uncom-fortable. "You're wrong." He raised his voice more than he needed to. "I know when to laugh, but I am definitely not funny. And I'm certainly not a 'funny guy.'" He shook his head back and forth for several seconds.

"Well, you remind me of a lot of funny people I know. Don't the kids laugh in your classes?" She pulled her chair up to the table and leaned her head on her hand.

"Sure, but I'm not funny." He meant it.

"But I bet you know what's funny. I bet things amuse you. What's the funniest thing that happened last year in school?" She was not going to stop.

What an odd question! But instead of telling her that he had to grade his papers, he just started talking. "Last fall in the middle of a class, out of the blue, a student raised her hand and said she thought it was great that we had a holiday honoring the doctors who took care of animals. She thought Veterans' Day was Veterinarians' Day."

"Veterinarians' Day!" Julie said. "Did you all laugh? I would have laughed."

"I tried not to, but after a while I cracked up. The class went crazy, of course. And Franny laughed, too. But I felt sorry for her, so we talked after class." In fact Armand was not sure that Franny understood her mistake. When he explained that a veteran was someone who had been in a war, she just shrugged.

Julie took a drink from her bottle. "Nice job. You didn't want to hurt her. I told you that you were funny." For a second Armand was afraid she was going to pinch his chin, but she just leaned back and smiled and asked for another story.

Within seconds he was describing a student production of *A Christmas Carol*. "It was directed by a first-year teacher who didn't know what he was doing, and it was a disaster. Near the end, Marley's ghost got his chain caught in the hot-air register. When he tugged, it stayed stuck and dust came up. People in the front row thought the auditorium was on fire."

Julie laughed hard. "Good stuff, Armand. I can see some pimply kid tugging at the chain while all the grandmothers in the audience sprint for the exits."

"That's pretty much what happened." He was pleased with her reaction.

"It must be great to have all that stuff in your head."

"Don't worry. When you're my age, you'll have plenty."

"I hope so. I hope what's in there will be funny." She paused and stared down at the table. "Got to go. I have a softball game at 5:50, and then I've got to grade papers." She lowered her voice into mock seriousness, "We'll continue this tomorrow." She patted him on the shoulder and hurried off.

Every afternoon they met after class in the empty cafeteria. She told him what she had done that day—always well planned, always well executed. He'd describe his class—lots of writing and discussion. Then they would leave together. They would usually stop at the 7-Eleven where he bought a large coffee. Then they walked to her apartment and sat on the porch swing where he told her funny stories. He told her about bringing the wrong tests to a final, about a freshman who sailed a desk out the window, about a student who threw up in the reserve room of the library, about a teacher who had been locked in the bathroom all night long.

She loved his stories, and he knew why. "How much easier with you than Bud," she must be thinking. "You're not an intense, young genius with sharp edges. You're well worn. Sure, you're getting bald, and you have a paunch, but so what? I like your world. I can see it." She might even have boyfriends who played softball with her and maybe drank beer and spent the night. But none of them could give her what Armand could. That's why she hung around him. And, of course, the school was empty. Who else could she talk to?

Sometimes they sat on the school lawn together. It was there that he told her about the sophomore who had once conducted an experiment by crossing out the C in COLD MILK to make it read OLD MILK. The student claimed a significant drop in milk sales. The same afternoon on the lawn, Armand recalled a time when one of his colleagues—to give his students real-life experience—invited them to steal everything in the building and bring it back to the class. They did. He almost lost his job.

Sometimes they would talk about her sports life, but almost always they came back to his stories. One of her favorites concerned a girl in a creative writing class. All semester long the girl had refused to turn in stories, promising to give him a 'complete work' in June. And she did: five stories copied from *Winesburg, Ohio*. Armand was astonished she had plagiarized so brazenly and a little hurt that she thought he wouldn't recognize such a well-known work. "I love it," Julie crowed. "I can't wait for my first plagiarist."

He remembered people he hadn't thought of in years. There was little Teddy Whitman, the introverted biology teacher from Butte, Montana. At faculty meetings, Teddy would nudge the man sitting next to him and nod in the direction of a female teacher. "See her?" he'd whisper. "I'd like to process her data." Or, "I'd like to lubricate her chassis," or "I'd like to tune her piano," or "I'd like to snake out her pipes." This continued until Teddy retired.

"What would Teddy say about me?" Julie asked. "Would he want to lubricate my chassis?" She was grinning.

"No comment." Armand felt uncomfortable.

"Don't look so embarrassed, Armand. Teddy would have noticed me, though. Wouldn't he?"

"Oh, yes. He would have noticed you." He paused and swallowed. No other words could come out.

"Okay," she laughed. "Tell me another story about a field trip."

And always she listened. "How could that happen?" she might ask. "Tell me that story again. I love it." And finally she would laugh—a long, sincere, lovely laugh, a laugh that told him how happy she was to be with him. And when she finally stopped laughing, she would keep on smiling.

The night before summer school ended, Armand sat in his study and made a long list of teaching memories. He started with the letter A. A could be Antonio, who used to sing in class, or A could be *All Quiet on the Western Front,* or the apricot someone stuck in his briefcase. For each letter, he jotted down memories until he had filled several pages. He was appalled at how much of himself he could pour out so quickly.

But then he thought about Julie. He could picture her rocking back and forth on the squeaky porch swing, eagerly prodding him to keep telling stores. Behind her was a lush green lawn and flowers. The smell of summer was everywhere. Soon he would have to imagine her somewhere else. But where? Where would she be? In the summer, they could leave together, and no one was there to notice. In the fall everyone would notice. Would she still come to his table? Would they sit next to each other at assemblies? Would she still want to hear funny stories? Would he have any to tell?

The next morning he taught his last class and then met Julie in the cafeteria. Before they said anything, a grinning man burst into the cafeteria and headed their way.

"Who's that?" Julie asked. The man had a gray beard, a green backpack, and a deep tan.

"Bob Hastings, another English teacher."

"Why the glum voice?"

"I didn't sleep last night."

Bob hurried over to them. "Armand, my boy! Who's the lady?" He pulled out a chair, turned it around, and straddled it. Armand introduced Julie.

"Here I go off fishing and hiking for the summer with my girlfriend, and the place falls apart." He pounded with mock anger on the table. "Do you realize, my dear, that no one sits at Armand's table."

"It's summer. Different rules, I guess. I enjoy hearing his funny stories." Her voice was scarcely inflected.

"Armand 'funny'? I suppose so. What have you been doing, Old Boy, watching *Comedy Central*? Does he tell you jokes after school too?" Hastings stretched out his arms.

"All the time—usually over at my place." Her voice flattened even more as she stared back at Hastings, who reached over and poked Armand in the neck. "Armand, you old devil, whatever have you been doing?"

Armand stared at his hands. "I'm funny in the summer, I suppose. Who would have guessed?"

"Honey," Hastings stood up and looked down at Julie, "one thing we all know is that this funny guy sitting next to you is the real thing. No one works harder. No one is better prepared." Then, as he started to edge away, "I'm back to pick up a few class lists, and that's it until September. So long, you two."

They walked home slowly and ended up on her swing. The humid weather made Armand feel especially tired.

"You look different," Julie announced after they sat down.

"I'm tired, Julie. And I don't really like this heat." The swing felt uncomfortable against his back. The wood scratched his bare legs.

"You're slouching. And your voice sounds kind of trembly."

"That's my old man's voice. Maybe I should get a ponytail to counteract it." He didn't feel like talking.

"It's not important." She shrugged and reached into her pocket for a stick of gum.

"Hastings is quite a guy," Armand said softly. "He can be very entertaining. Lots of energy."

"Hastings," she stopped chewing her gum, "is an asshole."

Armand ignored her. "Now there's someone with really funny stories. You'll find out next year." His words felt tight and stupid.

"Oh, please, Armand, please. The only thing I like about that phony is he gives me the courage to say what we've both been thinking for a long time."

"What's that?" Armand's stomach felt jumpy.

"Let's go inside," Julie said softly. "School's over for the summer. We've got other things to take care of, and you know it."

Armand heard himself breathe. His arms, already perspiring, felt even wetter. Had he ever felt more awkward?

"Julie," he stammered, "I have never thought about going to bed with you. I really haven't."

"Never? You have never thought about making love with me? You've never thought about us together?"

"Never in a serious way. I'm chasing retirement. You're just getting started. Believe me. You have made me funny; making love would not be funny."

"You'll do just fine." She put her hand on his knee. She didn't wear a ring or nail polish.

"I just can't." He moved her hand away. "Julie, I can't. I'm a funny guy remember? Not a sexy one."

"Can't you be both?"

"Obviously not."

She took the gum out of her mouth, balled it up, and tossed it on the lawn. He looked across the street. On the far sidewalk a man was reading a book while walking his dog. When he looked back she was on her feet and shaking her hands at her sides, as if she was loosening up for a marathon. Her eyes were glistening. "Coaches don't cry," she sniffed. "Coaches shouldn't cry."

"English teachers do all the time." He stood up awkwardly and put his hands behind his head. "I think I'll go to Wisconsin for the rest of the summer." He often rented a small place near Green Bay. Then he hugged her. She was solid, of course, but she also felt soft and for one second he thought about walking with her inside. But instead he pulled away his arm and walked across the lawn to the sidewalk and turned toward his apartment.

He stopped at Kelly's Tap for three scotches. Tim, the security guard, and a few of his buddies shouted to him from a table in the rear. Back home, he turned on the ball game and watched the Cubs lose in extra innings.

Armand parked his Toyota in the front lot, which had been closed all summer long. He noticed that the YOU ARE ENTERING COUGAR COUNTRY sign had been given a fresh coat of paint. For the first time since June he entered Forest High School through the front door. Inside he saw that the lockers had been repainted a bright red to match the school's colors. The trophy case along the far wall featured the trophy won by the girl's soccer team for placing third in the state last spring. A WELCOME CLASS OF 2013 banner hung over the doorway into the main classroom building. The floor, ferociously polished by Rocco and his crew, glistened like an ice rink. Without the hordes of teenagers, Forest High School smelled fresh and airy—but with a whiff of forbidden cigarette smoke.

"Hey, Mr. Waterman." It was Tim, the security guard. He was sitting on the bench with a *Weekly World News* in his lap. The headline read GIRL BORN WITH MONKEY HEAD. Tim was wearing a T-shirt with a faded picture of Bart Simpson skateboarding. He looked up and smiled at Armand. "Welcome back. How's the most respected teacher in the school?" He cupped a cigarette in his thick hand.

"I'm okay, Tim. But we saw a lot of each other this summer. You don't need to welcome me back." Tim had been Armand's student back in 1970, his first year as a teacher at Forest. Most of his class had gone on to college. Tim went to Vietnam. When he returned home, he tried to become a police officer but failed the exam three times. Then D.F. 'Porky' Boyd, the longtime Forest High School security guard, dropped dead while breaking up a fight after a basketball game. Superintendent Hayes believed in helping local kids—especially veterans—and he hired Tim to replace the 'Venerable Boyd.'

"I didn't forget about last summer." Tim coughed and pounded his chest. "I just like saying 'welcome back.' This was your first summer school ever wasn't it?" Tim knew things like that. He might be a bit thick, but he knew who taught where and when and sometimes even how.

"First and last." Armand paused and swallowed. "I had an interesting time, but summer should be spent on the golf course or at Wrigley Field. I was glad to help out, but no more."

"I hear we have a new English teacher." To cover his smile, Tim brought the cigarette to his mouth. He had pink, chapped skin and a belly that hung over his sweatpants. *In a few days,* Armand thought, *he will be wearing his uniform, which will make him appear more streamlined.*

"I don't know much about that, Tim." Armand hurried off down the hall. He half expected one more remark from Tim. He was certain that at this moment, his former student's chubby face had dropped into a gaping grin.

Rocco knew just how to set up his room. The desks were arranged in a semi-circle the way Armand liked them. The empty bulletin board was ready for his things. The flowers and plants along the windowsill were back and blooming. Those Italian janitors really knew how to keep things alive. From the closet he pulled out a box labeled SEPTEMBER. In it were posters of individual writers—Thoreau, Poe, Toni Morrison, Maya Angelou. Another poster had several smaller photos of Joyce, Synge, Yeats, Shaw, and other Irish writers. He knew where on the empty walls to tack each of these. In another part of the closet he found a large calendar, which he hung next to the bulletin board. The bulletin board itself would be used for announcements of movies, plays, and readings. It would also be the place for cartoons.

He pulled open the drawer of his desk. Inside were Cuban cigars Rocco had left for him. Instead of the cigars, he pulled out his lesson book for the year and opened it to page one. Once again he would plan the entire year from memory. In no time at all, it would all be written down—the classes, tests, papers, field trips. The old planning books were filed away just in case, but he never bothered to look at them. Any changes would be for the good. Normally, he never checked; this year he might have to. In the afternoon, he would study his class lists. Lately children of former students had been turning up in his classes. Later, he would meet Cummings for a steak. Cummings might fill him in on his summer travels. He was even closer to retirement than Armand.

On his way out of the school, Armand stopped in the office. He looked first at the general announcement board. Doreen Elders, a long-time Forest secretary, had died this summer. Colleagues were urged to send money to the lung cancer association. He wrote a short note thanking Rocco for the cigars and stuck it in Rocco's mailbox. In his own box was the agenda for the next day's meeting. And there was a letter from Greece. He

walked out of the office, down the hall, and out the building.
He stood on the front steps and opened the letter.

My Dear Armand,

I have taken a job in Athens. I think you'll agree this is a good idea.

Thanks for the summer, Funny Guy. I don't plan to forget you.

Love,

Julie

He hadn't figured she would leave the country. Of course,
she would know people in all those foreign places. They would
have schools and jobs for young teachers—especially ones who
could coach.

He considered buying a cup of coffee and walking down
Julie's street, but instead he sat down in the grass near a soccer
goal and looked back at the school. In July the two of them had
sat in the same spot, and he described Audrey pouring coffee
into his briefcase. He told Julie how he pulled out the soaked
papers one at a time and how he crouched in the bathtub drying
each sheet with Audrey's blow dryer.

They both laughed hard at that one, but now when he thought
about the two of them laughing together, all he could do was
wish that he was back in his classroom surrounded by hundreds
and hundreds of ungraded papers.

Ready or Not

Andy knew exactly where he was: just west of Wrigley Field. Sixty years ago when he was nine years old, he and his dad would have been a block away, trotting east on Waveland to get to the ballpark for batting practice. Once during batting practice a foul ball hit by his hero Hank Sauer dropped into his lap. And now, he was back in this bungalow neighborhood to pay his respects to the widow of Leo Benson, whom he had only known for three months. What was this guy's all-time favorite memory? Andy had no idea.

Bungalow. Andy always liked the word. Round and cozy—just like the place where his own grandparents had lived on South Paxton and later where his parents lived in Rogers Park before they moved to the big old house in Evanston. There were even bungalows near Forest High School, where Andy had taught for thirty-four years.

Benson's Bungalow. Perfect. You've got the two b's. Alliterative. Except that Benson was not round and cozy. He was bony and jagged and old and pointed. His hand, when you shook it, felt crab-like and slippery. Andy would always remember the first day Benson came to work at the GED office. A human stick, edging into their storefront place for the first day. A brittle little man. Sport coat with no tie. Briefcase and tennis shoes. Could have been an old elevator operator.

Two days from now at the funeral home, Andy would look down at him in the coffin. White and so absolutely still. But tonight he'd pay his respects to the man's wife and his family.

Why did Jack hire this old guy anyway? Jack had this feeling Benson could do it—even though he hadn't taught for years and even though his real job as an adult had been as a teller in a bank. Not even a loan officer. A teller. He sat behind the window and talked to customers. A teller. What in God's name do tellers tell?

Well, Jack had hired him. Jack, the old hippy radical—or was it a radical hippy? In the old days in California, he planned and led marches. Got himself arrested for destroying government property and later tried to go to Hanoi. He even cut sugar cane with Fidel and the boys. Now he was in his sixties and running a tiny GED center and hiring people like Andy and Benson to teach classes. But the trouble was that Benson was barely a teacher.

On the day of the hiring, Jack reminded the teachers for the zillionth time what they were all about. "Remember our students are ready. Your students will be ready. I'll find them, and you make sure they get what they are ready to get. Believe me. I know when they're ready. For them a GED is a new life. I think this old fellow Benson will be good at this kind of teaching. Trust me."

Well, they did trust Jack when it came to judging people. But still....

After all the years of marching and writing and appearing on panels as a grown-up child of the '60s, and after all those years with a ponytail and a radical reputation, Jack had decided to finish things off in a storefront GED office in Chicago's West Loop. And he had hired retired teachers like Andy, people who understood precisely what he wanted them to do. And they liked it. And why not? No administrators. No paperwork. Older students who wanted to learn. Not a bad way to spend the golden years in what was now being called an 'Encore Profession.'

Back at Forest High, Andy had taught the tough kids. In the evening, he worked with immigrants in Forest's night school program. A union guy. A couple of bad marriages. One good one and now a widower. Early retirement. Jack got Andy's name somewhere and gave him a call and they had lunch at Lou Mitchell's. Jack explained how he had finally decided to help people who could be helped, talk to people who are listening. Older people who don't want to fuck up the second time around. "Do you know people like this, Andy?"

"Yes, I do."

"Do you believe they can learn?"

"Yes, I do."

"You're hired," Jack smiled. "You'll like it here. And remember, they'll be ready."

And were they ever. Wanda was forty. Knocked up when she was sixteen. Lots of kids. Two boyfriends—one murdered and another in prison. A reader. A poet. Two languages. She was ready. No need to go to evening classes at the Y. She was ready, and Andy made sure she took the practice tests and worked on essay writing. He could do all of that. He could do the math. He could tell her what she needed to do to pass. He made sure she took the test. He even drove her to the testing site at Olive Harvey Community College on the far south side.

She passed the test with near-perfect scores, and Jack made a point of praising Andy. The other teachers were just as successful. Jack would find students who were ready. They would show up and be assigned a teacher. Andy usually got people like Wanda—older women, minorities. Nora worked with the ex-offenders. And Charles had the younger ones recently released from Juvenile Detention.

Jack was usually away from the office. He went to libraries, police stations, jails and anywhere else they might be. He put up signs. He even advertised on bowling score sheets. Some guy would be jotting down his score and look over and see the ad: ARE YOU READY TO MOVE ON?

Then Benson. "I've got this new guy," Jack said one day. "Benson. Retired fellow like you guys. Taught for two years and then worked in a bank. He says he wants to do this. He can do the work. Why not? Andy, I told him you could show him how this place works."

Yeah, Jack, why not? Only Benson wasn't ready to teach. He followed Andy around for a week. He observed the others and took notes like a madman. From the get-go, he seemed edgy and uncertain.

They gave him agreeable students like Betsy, who had already passed most of the test. All she needed was the math, and Benson helped her solve problems on the practice test. Basic stuff—percentages, fractions, a little bit of graphing. She learned enough and was all set to take the test. Then there was Barney, an older black guy who'd been in Vietnam. He needed his GED to qualify for his union pension. He had the whole thing memorized. Benson took him though some practice tests.

But it just didn't feel right, and as a lifelong teacher Andy had learned to trust his feelings. Why didn't Benson laugh more with the students? Why were things so serious over in his cubicle? Wouldn't the students want someone a little more human?

Andy was going to tell Jack the new guy was struggling. This might have been an exaggeration, but he would be struggling soon. No doubt about it. Still, he didn't feel like getting Jack involved.

Then Benson opened up a little. He got to work early to drink coffee and talk. He'd stay late and even have a beer. One afternoon, he told a story about a bank robbery. He said that some of the security people at the bank should know about this program.

But, to Andy, all this friendliness seemed forced. And Benson stayed silent when the conversation got raunchy. How could he have not been awfully uncomfortable with a bunch of politically incorrect retired people who'd laugh at anything? What was Benson supposed to think when Lois—crazy, tattooed Lois— announced that she had been driving to work behind a nerdy little guy on a motor scooter. When she got close, she could see that the back of his shirt read: IF YOU CAN READ THIS, THE BITCH FELL OFF. Lois went nuts. "Can you believe that little fucker had a T-shirt that says that? I love it!" Benson smiled and nodded, but he looked pained.

It was the same thing when Maurice told the group about his new student Bea Gomez, who talked about herself in the third person. If she had a question she'd say, "Bea don't know." Benson tried to laugh, but he must have wondered how anyone could make fun of the people they were teaching.

This went on for another month. Benson seemed to be okay with the teaching, but he didn't have a clue when it came to relating to his students or to the others. Was this a good way for him to spend retirement? The others agreed that he was probably uncomfortable, but they didn't seem to worry that much.

Well, Andy did. He'd have a conversation with Benson. It wasn't his job to fire the old guy, but he could tell him why he thought he wasn't quite right for the job. He'd compliment him on his efforts and suggest some other places that might be better. A man-to-man chat. The right thing to do.

Two days later, the day that Andy was going to take Benson to Starbucks, a call came for him at the office. "Andy, this is Leo Benson's wife, Alice. I've got sad news. My husband died last night. He had a heart attack. You might want to stop by. He so admired you—"

Andy saw a woman come to the window, part the curtains and look out. Then the front door of the bungalow opened, and there she was gesturing for him to come in.

Alice was short and erect with gray hair. She spoke in a clear, forceful voice. A serious-looking lady with intense eyes. Hard to slip bullshit past her. Benson had told them one day that she worked for a patent lawyer in the Loop and never, ever missed a day of work.

On the way into the house Andy told her how sorry they all were. His wife had died last year and he knew how she felt. Alice nodded and touched his arm. "He had a bad heart. It was going to happen. So nice of you to come. He liked all of you so much. Such a great thing for him to do at his age."

The living room had two couches, several chairs and bookshelves, thick rugs and a polished wooden floor. Photographs of old people covered one wall, and there was a small fireplace with a small fire. It smelled slightly of soup cooking.

"These are some of our relatives," she said. They all stood and shook hands, and he sat down on a couch near the fireplace. Alice sat on one side and Gus, Benson's brother from the south side, sat on the other.

"Will there be a lot of people at the funeral?"

"Some, not a lot," Alice said. "We have a small family. No children and only a small group of friends. But it will be attended. I'm sure the bank will have people there. He was at the bank for almost forty years. And maybe some customers. People knew him. He was the teller, the first person they saw. He always had treats for the dogs that people tied up in front. He knew all the dogs' names. And the teachers from your GED Center—they'll probably be there."

Gus spoke in a crisp, Chicago voice. He worked for the Department of Sanitation. He retired young with a heart problem. "Runs in the family," he said. "Benson was the smart one. Our parents had wanted him to be a professor. He liked the research, but he knew he wouldn't be happy with the college crowd. He was awfully shy. Then he tried teaching little kids, and that didn't work. Wrong age. Then the bank."

Gus paused, and Alice started talking again. "Jack told me about your little school."

"You know Jack?"

She smiled. "He was here last night. He and I marched together in California. We knew each other very well. When he moved to Chicago, I was the first person he called. Last year he asked me if I knew anyone who was ready for a GED. I said I didn't, but Benson was retired and might like to teach GED."

"So it was your idea," Andy said.

"It was," she said. "But Jack liked it. He knew Benson had taught. He knew he worked hard and that he was a good listener. Jack said sometimes in retirement we try what we never quite tried earlier in our lives."

Andy's mind wandered to his own could-have-beens: college teaching, law, baseball, social work?

Gus asked about the students. Andy told them about Cyrus. Older guy. Black. Great reader. He wants to be a lawyer. He learned to argue in prison. Twice a week, he showed up with a completed practice test. After going over it with him, Andy gave him essay questions, and he wrote essays right there.

"Are they good?" Gus wondered.

"Good enough. He can stick to a point."

"He's ready?" Gus asked.

"Oh, yeah." It was easy for Andy to talk about this. He could go on for a long time.

"Alice," he suddenly asked, "was Benson a radical?"

"A radical teller." She smiled. "No, not at all. Never."

"So you didn't meet at a peace rally?"

"We met in our thirties. I had started at the law firm; he had left teaching to work at the bank. Friend fixed us up. On our first

date, we went to see a play at the Goodman. We had a comfortable life in this bungalow."

Andy could imagine Benson sitting where he was sitting now.

"Let me show you his office." He followed her down the hall
past a bedroom, through the kitchen and down a short flight of
stairs to the basement. In the corner against the wall was a desk
half enclosed by bookshelves. Andy walked over. One shelf had
stacks of *Wall Street Journals* and *Forbes* magazines. On the other
shelf were GED books and grammar and usage books. There
were also several teaching memoirs and books of educational
philosophy.

On the wall was a pencil sketch with Benson's initials at the
bottom. Obviously the work of an amateur, but not bad. What
he had drawn was easily identifiable—the faculty at Jack's little
GED place. There was Lois with her tattoos and Stuart with his
mustache and Arthur with his modified Afro and Jenny with her
beret. In the middle was Jack with his ponytail and there was
Andy—short and dark and squinting. And between Jack and
Andy with his arms draped over their shoulders and a big grin
on his face stood a youthful Benson. And he was smoking.

"He was serious about this program." Alice had stepped up
beside him. "He had spent a lifetime thinking about schools.
He didn't like the idea of teaching in college. Little kids were
exhausting. But folks who were almost there struck him as
interesting. These were his people. He found this all incredibly
exciting. I could tell even though he didn't talk about it much."

Andy couldn't take his eyes off the sketch. "We could tell too,"
he finally said. "He fit right in. He was one of us."

Headmaster

"I told you not to mention Marvin when Richardson is over."
Babs, in her faded blue robe with her hair flopped over her
shoulders, smoking a cigarette, glared across the room at Brad,
who was standing next to the dining room table. It was breakfast time, but the dishes from the previous night's dinner party
had not been cleared. Cigarettes floated in the tops of several
glasses. The lamb gravy had congealed.

"What could I do," Brad answered automatically, "ignore him?
Richardson wanted to know what Marvin had been doing since
leaving Guilford, and I told him. So let's drop it, okay?"

Babs wasn't going to drop it. After being married to her for
twenty years, he knew that much—she would not drop it. Brad
yawned and waited for her to go on.

"You must have brayed on for eight minutes. I could feel you
gloating." She changed the pitch of her voice to mimic his.
"'Marvin turned down the job at Andover and other fancy prep
schools; Marvin took a job at a public school in the city; Marvin
led an antiwar protest; Marvin spoke out against the Boston
mayor for cutting school spending.' Everything you said reminded
Richardson that Marvin thinks prep schools are silly."

Brad cleared his throat. "That wasn't what I meant."

"It wasn't? Does Richardson need to be reminded of how
remote we are here at Guilford?"

Instead of saying anything Brad turned toward the window
and looked outside. "Look," he blurted, "Sally Hopkins is riding
by on her bike. I thought we kicked her out of school."

"We gave her a second chance," Babs snapped. "We decided
she needed this school more than she needed to live at home

with her demented family." Babs picked up one of the glasses from the night before and swallowed its contents. Brad wondered if it was a glass with a cigarette.

"Wasn't my committee supposed to be consulted?" Brad had been a member of the Faculty Review Committee ever since he and Babs arrived at Guilford School twelve years before. No student could be expelled or reinstated without passing through the Review Committee.

"We had to act fast. All of you were grading final exams. No one gives a shit about your committee anyway."

"And Richardson said we could give Sally another chance?"

"Headmaster Richardson will do whatever I ask," she said, making her voice as bored as possible. "I *am* the counselor. Actually, I left a memo on my desk and figured he would read it. He reads everything I leave there." She shook out her blond hair, stood up from the table and leaned forward. "I'm going to shower. Why don't you find someplace else to nap today? I want to be alone. I'm not going to forgive you for talking so much about Marvin. You know, you can be good company and you're not a bad teacher, but you can also be a real prick."

A real prick. He was a lot of things, but he wasn't a real prick. Brad decided this as he walked from his house across the football-field-sized quad towards Guilford Library. He liked the Guilford School in June. Only a handful of students attended summer school. He would teach in the mornings and in the afternoon write or ride his bike or walk through the country. This is what prep school teaching was supposed to be. Much better than Forest High, the public school outside of Chicago where he used to teach and where he met Babs. They taught together for a year but then headed to the East for jobs at Guilford—where she could be close to her family and their money.

Marvin's former house loomed on the right. It was a two-story Tudor, just like all the other Masters' houses. On the day the U.S. invaded Iraq, Marvin hung a huge GET OUT OF IRAQ NOW! banner from the window. It dangled there for two weeks. Even the people who didn't like the banner wouldn't dare tell Marvin to take it down. Brad had wondered if it might cause trouble, but he didn't bother to say anything and knew Babs would be furious if he did. She had taken a picture of it on the day she was taking pictures of Marvin's classes for the yearbook. She didn't submit the picture to the yearbook, but she did give it to Marvin.

Babs was right, of course. He didn't have to go on about Marvin at dinner. A simple 'He's teaching in Maine' would have been sufficient. Even a shrug and a smile might have worked. What he said had definitely hurt Richardson.

But Brad had always talked about Marvin, ever since he and the other members of the Hiring Committee had reported back to Richardson that Marvin would be a strong English teacher, the kind they were looking for. He might have wrinkled clothes and shaggy hair, but this guy was sharp. The next day Ricardson himself interviewed Marvin, and the day after that he was hired.

As a first-year teacher at Guilford, he was all Brad had predicted. He also became Brad's buddy. Babs and Marvin's wife didn't have much to say to each other, but 'the boys' hit it off. Back in Chicago for vacations, Brad would tell their old friends all about Marvin—touch football, tennis, smoking pot, hiking. At first Babs would join in with the Marvin stories, and she could be funny, much funnier than Brad. But on one of the trips back to Chicago she stopped talking about Marvin. That was about the time Marvin decided he didn't like touch football after all.

Brad neared the library, but instead of walking inside he sat on the steps and looked back across the campus. Before he knew

it, he had started to snooze, a peaceful summer morning nap
brought on by an ever-so-slight hangover.

"Hello, Brad." He had not seen Headmaster Richardson walk
up behind him and sit down. Even on a Monday morning in
June, a week before the start of summer school, Richardson, tall
and thin with a leathery face, still wore a sport coat with leather
patches on the elbows, and carried a pipe—the typical headmaster look, the one Brad described to people who had never met
the Headmaster. But today, Brad was more aware of Richardson's
shaky hands and stooped posture. He looked more like a tired,
beaten man than a typical headmaster. Must be the hangover.
Richardson sat down on the stairs close to Brad.

"Good meal last night, my man. Babs can really cook lamb.
And you continue to be the master of the martini. Before, during
and after dinner—a martini evening with the Fosters."

"I thought it would be good to celebrate the end of school and
all that. But I'm afraid my hand was rather heavy with the drinks
last night." They both stared across the way, not at each other.

"No apologies, Brad. I'm a big boy. When my wife was alive,
I would always stop drinking after dinner, but now at times like
these, with people you know, who cares?" He paused for a moment
and sucked in his breath. "You heard about the Hopkins girl?"

"We let her back in."

"I let her back in after Babs told me more about her family.
Babs also said she had done exceptionally well in Marvin's class.
She has to do well in summer school. But she's in as far as I'm
concerned."

"Should my committee meet to discuss her?"

"You'll have to, but give her a chance, Brad. She'll be in your
class next year. But we'll talk about that later." He sucked on his
pipe, and then started up again in a slightly lower voice. "I was
interested in hearing about Marvin last night."

"You probably heard more than you needed to. I'm afraid I rattled on." Brad stood up and pretended to stretch and then sat down a few feet away.

"As I said about your martinis, I'm a big boy. I can stand hearing about him. I miss him, actually."

"You do?" Brad did not have to fake his surprise. "Even after the meeting last year?"

"Even after that infamous faculty meeting. I understand you can act the whole thing out."

"What, what do you mean?" Brad stammered.

"You know what I mean. No, I miss him because I miss him. I liked the way his classes went, even the unruly ones. I liked the notes he sent to the kids. In many ways, he was the real thing. I thought the picture Babs took of him for the yearbook said it all. On the lawn in a circle of his students, just laughing. Marvin knew how to laugh."

"But after the meeting—?"

"After the meeting I went home and vomited. Then I drank a bottle of vodka. I seriously thought about getting in my car and driving forever. I couldn't imagine ever working here again."

Brad had never discussed the meeting with the headmaster. "Were you surprised?"

"Surprised? Of course. Have you ever felt yourself being publicly ripped apart? What do you English teachers call it, *excoriated?*" Across the way Brad could see Babs standing in front of their house smoking a cigarette. "He called me the weakest person he had ever seen. He said I embarrassed him. I made teaching a scummy profession."

Brad remembered the meeting perfectly. Marvin had asked the headmaster why he had removed a book—*Being There* by Jerry Kozinsky—from the required list. Richardson had explained that teachers could still teach the book. He just didn't want it on the

list. He mumbled something about a masturbation scene that
made one of the older board members nervous. "The Duncan
family, as you know, has supported us for years." That's when
Marvin had gone crazy. He leaped to his feet pointing and
shouting.

"What hurt the most, of course, was the precision. Headmas-
ters learn to be hypocrites. It's almost a compliment. But he was
so gruesomely particular in what he said about me—my upbeat
speeches to the students, sucking up to parents, trying to lead
cheers at soccer matches. He must have spent time studying me.
I knew him well. He saw me as a complete loser. Not anyone
to take seriously." He paused and turned to look at Brad. "Does
that come through when you act out the scene?"

"I—"

"And what were you thinking at that meeting, Brad? You
agreed to remove the book. He was attacking you too, wasn't he?"

"I suppose."

"You suppose. You *know* he was. But he didn't attack you
because he wanted to go after me."

Brad looked over at a small statue of one of the school's
founders. It was on the lawn near the library steps.

"But still," Richardson continued, "you could have jumped in."

"I—"

"Next time. Right, Brad?"

Brad decided not to answer. He stared at his sandals and
watched his fingers beat a small tattoo on his knees. He could
hear Richardson wheezing. He didn't have to look at him to
know that he was tapping his teeth with the stem of his pipe.
"Don't worry, Brad. It's all over."

"It's good," Brad finally managed to half whisper. "We probably
should have talked about this before."

"You did me a favor talking about him last night. But now it's over. Now we start summer school. Now we keep the Hopkins girl around. Now you teach *Silas Marner* one more time."

"I love summer school."

"I have to walk to town, Brad. Do me a favor and make my calls. You'll see a list on my desk. You've done this before. Let the summer staff know when they're supposed to be here. Call the gardener. It's all on the list."

The list was on the desk near the phone and next to a picture of Richardson and his family. Evie had been a friendly, harmless sort of person, nothing like the daughter who stood on the right. An only child, she had attended Guilford but never really liked it. She worked as a waitress in Sacramento, living alone and out of touch with her father. She had not been home for two years.

Sometimes Brad liked snooping at Richardson's stuff, but not today. His hangover had grown worse since the conversation on the library steps. Make the calls, he thought, and find a quiet place to sleep. The hammock behind the gym should do just fine. Brad had left many a hangover on the hammock.

He had just started calling Mr. Allegretti, the gardener, when he noticed it. In fact, if he had been sharper, he would have noticed it immediately because it was right there next to the list. It was a letter, and Richardson had left it there to be read.

Marvin,

You were right. Enough's enough. But I still miss seeing you, especially now with B the only show in town. But I'm sure I'll find someone else. I always do.

The letter wasn't signed, but her handwriting was all too familiar.

The Caddy

I'm a caddy. I used to work as a runner for guys trading pork bellies and other crap at the Board of Trade, but I hated those people. How can you respect morons in odd-colored jackets squealing and shoving and making silly hand signals? Those guys really thought they were something special. But I knew they weren't. The Exchange was one huge pit full of kids. They were all kids, even the old ones. It makes me want to vomit just to think about them. I could have strangled every one of them.

Now at Pine Acres, where I caddy, you find adults, not guys bent over bathroom sinks cutting lines of coke with their plastic ID cards. You find confident men who move slowly, even when they have somewhere they need to be. And they always smile. They smile at me and the other caddies. They smile at the black guys and the Mexicans who work in the kitchen. They smile at each other. Not big, toothy grins, just simple smiles.

I love everything about the place. That's why I came back. I love standing all alone in the bag room at night. It's dark in there except for a little light reflecting off the metal clubs. It smells of leather and earth. In the whole world, there's nothing like the smell of the bag room at a country club. Once when I was a young caddy, I spent the whole night in the bag room. I waited until my mother was asleep and then I sneaked out of our apartment back to the club and climbed through the window. I curled up next to a huge black leather bag and made a pillow out of some club covers. I still go in there any chance I get. Anyway, I see caddying as real work. And I get to meet the finest people you can find anywhere—people like Mr. Roger Burrows.

There's a picture of Mr. Burrows on the wall of the men's grill. It was taken after a special golfing event. It shows a bunch of men sitting around the pool sipping gin and tonics. Most of them are wearing green pants or yellow pants with light blue blazers. They look tanned and freshly showered. The tables have bowls of chips and smaller containers of dip. A black waiter in a white coat is standing behind. Mr. Burrows is off to the side looking past the men sitting next to him. He's wearing black slacks with a green shirt and a light sport coat.

Mr. Burrows and I knew each other at Forest High School. But after he went to Princeton and I went to work, we didn't see each other. Some time after I had given up the bag the first time, he joined Pine Acres—just like his parents.

"Remember me?" I asked him the first time I caddied for him. We were walking down the fairway of the first hole. I had to hurry to keep up with his long strides.

He slowed down just a bit and turned to look at me. "Arthur? Arthur? My God, of course I do! We played football together in high school." I can still picture myself in that green Pine Acres T-shirt with the big bunker behind me. Mr. Burrows was looking right at me, not at anything else in the whole world.

At thirty-two he was already graying just a bit. But he still looked like the running back I used to block for—broad shoulders, strong jaw, big forearms, deep intense eyes. My mother remembered those eyes. She used to clean his family's house. She said the whole family joked about Roger's eyes. "They're staring all the way from Chicago to Princeton," they'd say.

He asked me if I'd been a caddy for a long time, and I told him how I'd caddied at Pine Acres through high school and that I had come back after my rotten experience at the Exchange. He told me that lots of people our age were caddying. We both shrugged. Then he lowered his voice and kind of smiled and said, "Maybe some day I'll quit the bank and join you."

By now we had reached his drive and I handed him a five iron. We both stopped talking as he lined up the shot. He waggled the club a few times and then started his backswing. He had a nice full swing with a complete follow through. The ball landed on the green and bounced backwards.

For the rest of that round we jabbered on about high school. He said that when we played football, he liked to run to the right because he knew I'd always clear the way for him. He didn't seem surprised that I was still living at home. A few holes later he had me shake hands with the others in the foursome. "If you ever need help, Arthur here is your man," he said. One man in the foursome, a fat bald guy, made a point of not looking at me when he shook my hand.

On the way back to the clubhouse after the eighteenth hole, I asked if I still could call him Mr. Burrows.

"If that's easier, fine. But I get to call you Arthur."

"That's the way it should be."

On the way to the clubhouse, we talked about his game. If he played in the club championship, he wanted me to carry the bag. He had broken 80 for the first time that summer.

It was that way all summer. If I wasn't out on a loop already, I would caddy for Mr. Burrows. I got to know his game. The four times he shot in the seventies, I was his man. He'd ask for advice, and I'd give it to him. When he was having trouble in the bunkers, I told him to keep his weight forward. On long irons, I had him line up a little bit left and throw his arms out towards the target. I could get him to slow down if he was getting too excited. He would never putt until I had given him my opinion about the green.

What I really liked about Mr. Burrows was that he could see all the way through bullshit. This one time the others in his foursome were talking about alcoholics. I guess someone in the club had just joined a dry-out program or something and had gone off to some place in Minnesota. Then one of the other players came out with the crap you hear all the time about not being able to help someone unless 'he wants to be helped.' Now if you think about that statement, it's pretty stupid. In the first place, people say it because other people have said it. They haven't really thought up the words themselves. But people still nod and frown like something smart has been said. And it's bullshit. Who says you can't make someone stop drinking? And how can you tell what people *want* to do? Anyway, on this afternoon, this guy frowned, lowered his voice, and announced, "You know, it doesn't do any good to help a drinker unless he wants to be helped." Everyone else—even the other caddies— nodded like pigeons and mumbled. Not Mr. Burrows. He just studied the scorecard and didn't say one word. He might have known my dad was a drinker, who would have been better off if someone had kicked his ass until he stopped.

After caddying, I usually stopped at the Wonder Bar for shots and beer. I didn't have any friends at the club. Most of the caddies were much younger. They wouldn't want to hang out with a thirty-two-year-old. And their parents wouldn't be too hot on the idea either. I'd sit there and drink beer and think about what I had done that day. And I'd always think about Mr. Burrows. Sometimes I'd drive past his house on the way home from the bar so I could imagine his life better. He lived in a big brick place back in the woods. And I knew what his wife and kids looked like because they would hang around the pool. Her name was Henrietta. She was tall and handsome. And I guess very rich. A waitress told me that Mr. Burrows met her at a party on Long Island.

One time I took a short cut from the caddy shack to the parking lot, and on the way I passed the swimming pool. Mr. Burrows and his family were there but sitting off in the corner. She was on a lounge chair reading a big book. Mr. Burrows was sitting on the deck near her. It looked like he was doing a crossword puzzle. The daughters, who were handsome like their mother, were sitting on towels playing cards. No one looked too happy.

In late August things slowed down. The weather turned hot and humid. A lot of caddies went back to school. I was often the only guy at the club carrying bags. One afternoon I was watching a ball game in the caddy shack, and Mr. Burrows walked in and came right over to me. "Let's play nine, Arthur," he said. "We'll carry our own bags." I looked at the caddy master, but he just shrugged a "Why not?" and we went off and played. I figured it would be awkward for a few holes, but then it would be fun. I wanted Mr. Burrows to see how far I could drive a golf ball. But he was off somewhere else, and I could barely get him to talk. After seven holes, it started raining, and we left. In the parking lot he apologized for being so gloomy. I said it was gloomy weather. Then we got into our cars and drove away.

In September, Mr. Burrows played a few rounds with a man named Ben Flowers. It seemed strange because Ben was not really Burrows' type—or anyone's, for that matter. In the first place, he had to be at least seventy-five years old. He wore shiny pants. He talked during the game. He had a terrible sense of humor. And he was mean. A few years ago, he got a caddy fired for laughing. My mother never liked working for people like that. She warned me, "Watch out for the mean old men. They'll hurt you." But I bet that prick was a mean young man too. No wonder he never married.

The caddy master told me that Mr. Burrows had worked for
Flowers at the First National Bank, and when Flowers retired,
he took over most of his accounts. In the winter Flowers lived in
some old people's place in Florida; in the summer he stayed in
Chicago. This fall he was actually living in an apartment owned
by Pine Acres. Even though he and Mr. Burrows belonged to
the same club, they looked more like two strangers who happened to be walking alongside each other. They were like people
who leave the train together. They have nothing in common
except the ride.

The Club Championship was played the last weekend in
August, and Mr. Burrows decided to enter. I thought maybe he
had gone East with his family because I hadn't seen his wife and
kids at the pool. But it turned out he'd stayed behind, and that's
when he started playing golf with Ben Flowers all the time. With
almost all of the other caddies gone, I carried their bags every
day. They would play at odd times; it seemed like we were the
only ones on the course. Once a guy playing alone joined us,
but usually it would just be the three of us—Mr. Burrows, Mr.
Ben Flowers, and me carrying two bags. Autumn was coming,
and the leaves would soon begin to fall, and there's nothing
worse than trying to find a golf ball in the leaves.

Things got uncomfortable fast, especially when they started
playing for $50 a hole. Sometimes people play for money, but
not for that much. But the season was over, so no one would
notice anyway. Mr. Burrows was a much better golfer so he had
to give Flowers a stroke on practically every hole.

A few days later things took a real ugly turn. As we were
walking down the first fairway, Flowers started talking into Mr.
Burrow's left ear. He would stop occasionally to spit and then
catch up with Mr. Burrows and grab him by the elbow and start
jabbering again. I couldn't quite hear what he was saying, but

I could hear the old man kind of giggling. Every so often he would poke Mr. Burrows in the ribs and cackle. Once he said something and looked over at me and grinned. I just stared back at the wrinkled little bastard. Mr. Burrows stopped walking and just shook his head. He had a pained look on his face. I really felt sorry for him, but I couldn't do anything. It wasn't like football where I could make the block to spring him loose.

On the back nine that day, Flowers started saying things to me, but he made sure Mr. Burrows heard him. Did I know that Mr. Burrows worked for him when he first came to the bank? Did I know that Mr. Burrows was a real party boy back in the early days? He said 'boy' with kind of a smirk. Did I know some of the 'special' bars that he used to go to? Had I ever seen any pictures of him dancing? The stuff didn't make any sense to me, but Flowers laughed so hard he was snorting. Mr. Burrows just walked on ahead with his hands stuffed in his pants. I stared at the grass and wished I was somewhere else. At the end of the match Mr. Burrows paid Flowers $100 and walked off to the parking lot without even saying goodbye to me. That had never happened before.

The nastiness got even worse a few days later. On the first tee Mr. Flowers bumped into me and then stuck his face right onto mine. He had yellowish pink skin with dark liver spots. One eye had a lot of mucus in it. And he wore this little gold chain around his chicken neck. He reeked of bourbon and cigarettes. "Arthur, I don't want any more fuck-ups today. When I'm putting, keep your mouth shut."

I started to say something, but he just laughed and walked away and I stared at the ground. People don't say things like that at our club. And I never talk when people are putting. Mr. Burrows heard it all and tried to make a joke, but he knew how

I felt. Flowers must have been drunk, though, because he forgot it right away.

For the rest of the round, he taunted Mr. Burrows. They were playing for even bigger money. Flowers would whisper things during his shots. Once I looked over and they were pointing fingers at each other. I looked back again and Flowers had his arm around Mr. Burrows' shoulder, and Burrows was squirming to get loose. Finally on the fifteenth hole, Flowers lost his ball in the woods. He claimed he'd found it, but he had obviously dropped another one. I was his caddy, for Christ's sake. I knew he was using a Pinnacle. But he picked up a Titleist that he swore was his. He had a shot to the green and ended up somehow winning the hole. When we were walking to the next green, he was whispering in Mr. Burrows' ear. Then he reached into the pocket of his plaid pants and pulled out a color picture. Mr. Burrows took one look at it and marched off to the club-house. Flowers shrugged and said, "I think I'll quit too. Come on, Arthur. Let us follow our manchild back to the bar."

The next day—yesterday—we were on the first tee ready to play again. Flowers was moving more steadily. They had agreed to play for less money. I had never seen Mr. Burrows play better. After seven holes he was one under par, and I think the pressure was affecting him less than me. I was really excited for him. He was quiet. He made a point of walking down the fairway near me. Flowers was off by himself. One time Flowers cheated, but no one said anything. By the ninth hole, Mr. Burrows had slipped over par, but he was still playing great. At this rate he was going to be in the low seventies.

On hole number twelve he was still just one over par. It was a short hole, just 140 yards. This would be perfect for Mr. Burrows' nine iron. Right before he started to swing, Flowers started talking frantically. "Roger, does Arthur here know that there have been other Arthurs in your life? Have you told him about Terry? Have you told him where you got the money to get darling Terry to vanish?" Flowers had this crazy smirk all over his face. He was leaning on his club in a way that made him look like an old sheepherder. Mr. Burrows stared right at him. His jaw was moving a little. It looked like his eyes were about to explode. He looked down at the ball and then swung wildly. It shot off to the left into the trees, and that was it. He ended up shooting an 84. I felt terrible for him because this was going to be his day.

Afterward, they both went to the bar. I went back to the caddy shack. I was just about to leave when the phone rang.

"Arthur?" It was Mr. Burrows. His voice sounded tight. "I'd like you to do me a favor."

"Of course, sir. Whatever you want."

"Ben and I are going to stay here at the bar for a while. I don't want him driving home. He's already finished off five martinis. I thought it would be better if he left his car here and you walked him home through the woods. He lives in one of those apartments on the other side of the course."

"I know just where it is. A lot of retired members stay over there."

"That's right. Come over to the bar door at ten o'clock. We'll be the only people at the club so it won't look funny for a caddy to be standing there. When we leave, I'll hand you Ben. You can take him by the arm and escort him to the woods. He won't have much to say."

"I'll get him home. No problem."

"One more thing, Arthur." He hesitated for a long time. "I want you to pick up something from my car. It's in the glove compartment. Make sure you do it before you walk him home. Thanks for everything, buddy. You're the best person I know."

I knew where Mr. Burrows parked his Lexus. I looked to make sure no one thought I was breaking in. Then I opened the passenger door and sat down. The car had a warm, leathery feeling to it. It reminded me of the bag room. It was empty except for some books in the back seat. I guess Mr. Burrows liked to read. I pushed the button of the glove compartment. The little door came down slowly the way they do on good cars. On my cars they always flop down like they have been dropped from the sky. Inside I could see the title to the Lexus, the insurance forms, and some maps. Below the maps something glistened. It was a hunting knife, and even before I touched it, I knew it would be razor sharp.

Bob Boone started teaching in 1964. He has taught in Staten Island, Germany, Highland Park, and Chicago. In 1991, he founded Young Chicago Authors to provide opportunities for young writers from the city.

He has written several textbooks, a teaching memoir, and a sports biography. This is his first work of fiction.

He lives in Glencoe, Illinois, with his wife Sue. He has three children and five grandchildren.

Made in the USA
Monee, IL
21 August 2022

11197206R00057